True North

Susan Diane Johnson

True North

Contact Information: titleadmin@pelicanbookgroup.com

Cover Art by *Nicola Martinez*

Harbourlight Books, a division of Pelican Ventures, LLC
www.pelicanbookgroup.com PO Box 1738 *Aztec, NM * 87410

Harbourlight Books sail and mast logo is a trademark of Pelican Ventures, LLC

Publishing History
First Harbourlight Edition, 2014
Electronic Edition ISBN 978-1-61116-295-0
Print Edition ISBN 978-1-61116-311-7
Published in the United States of America

Dedication

To my son, Kirk, who inspired this book with his dream of seeing orca whales in the sea instead of in an aquarium. To my mother, Barbara, who gave us the trip that made his dream happen. To my husband, Keith, for all the nights eating pizza so I can write. I love you all so much.

Praise

Under the title *Northern Lights* this novel won the following awards: The Maggie, The Lone Star, and The Beacon.

Acknowledgements

My wonderful critique partners, Stacy Monson and Narelle Atkins challenge me and make my writing better.

My father, Bill, and my sister, Pam, encourage me and give me unconditional love.

My dear friends Sharon Gillenwater and Diane Langley pray with me, cry with me, and laugh with me. They are truly two gifts from God.

My Inkwell Inspirations blog partners and sisters in Christ have been a daily source of prayer, friendship, and encouragement for three years. I'm so blessed to have each of them in my life.

I'm also blessed to have Fay Lamb, Nicola Martinez, and Barbara Early as my editors. Their exceptionally brilliant input has taught me so much and has made this into a far better book.

"Therefore we do not lose heart. Though outwardly we are wasting away, yet inwardly we are being renewed day by day. For our light and momentary troubles are achieving for us an eternal glory that far outweighs them all. So we fix our eyes not on what is seen, but on what is unseen. For what is seen is temporary, but what is unseen is eternal."

~2 Corinthians 4:16-18 (NIV)

Prologue

"Cody, are you almost ready?" Lisa Kendall glanced at the clock sitting on the entryway table. Shaped like a catcher's mitt with a baseball in the center, it reflected most of the décor in their house. Baseball topped her nine-year-old son's list of passions. Whales and anything to do with the ocean took a close second, so both themes ran throughout the Kendall household. Not that she minded one bit. There would be plenty of time to decorate the house *her* way when Cody grew up and went off to college.

"Your dad should be home any minute." She glanced at the clock again then out at the driveway and tried to stem her rising tension level. Joe promised he wouldn't let their son down today, of all days. Today Cody's Little League team would play their final game of the season. Cody wanted his dad to be there for at least one of his games.

While Lisa would like to believe the sincerity of her husband's promise, it looked like work would take precedence over family. Again.

"Just a sec, Mom. I'm getting my glove. Oops."

A crash came from the direction of Cody's room, followed by the slamming of the door and the sound of feet scrambling down the hall. Cody skidded to a halt in front of her.

"OK, I'm ready." He looked up at her and beamed, proudly dressed in his red and white pinstriped baseball uniform. His brown eyes and quirky smile were a miniature version of Joe's. Small in stature, like Lisa, he also had her blonde hair. But the smattering of freckles across Cody's face belonged to no one but Cody. Lisa felt the same catch in her heart she always did when her son smiled at her. She simply couldn't imagine life without this precious little boy.

"What fell over in your room?"

"Just my stack of whale books. Nothing got hurt, though. I'll pick 'em up when we get home."

Lisa bit back a smile. She'd been after Cody to put those books on a shelf for weeks. Nodding, she peered out the window. Still no sign of Joe.

"I don't think Dad's gonna come to my game."

Something inside Lisa wrenched at Cody's matter-of-fact tone. He seemed way too comfortable with Joe's long hours at work. More used to it than any little boy should ever have to be.

Which of Joe's divorce cases interfered with his family time today? Though tired of Joe's long hours at the law firm, she instantly regretted the direction of her thoughts. Joe worked hard in a demanding profession to provide the best life he could for them. Not only that, he agonized over his extra time at work as much as she did. "Forgive me, Lord." She took a deep breath and prayed for help with her attitude.

"Hey, Mom, you're wearing the shirt!"

"I sure am, sweetheart. It's my lucky shirt."

Cody grinned, and Lisa's heart filled with joy. The sweatshirt depicted an orca swimming on the ocean floor. Cody drew the picture when he was in the first grade, after a trip to the Vancouver Aquarium in British Columbia. At that time, they still had orcas in the aquarium.

Cody had fallen truly and madly in love.

Surprisingly though, the picture he'd drawn after the trip wasn't of an orca in an aquarium. Rather, the whale swam along the ocean floor, surrounded by seaweed, starfish, and shells. Cody declared all whales belonged in the ocean and not the aquarium.

Lisa loved the picture so much she made a copy, stenciled it onto two sweatshirts then painted one for her and one for Cody. She wore hers proudly, and Cody always seemed to get a kick out of it when she wore it in public.

"We'd better go. Otherwise the coach will make me sit out the first half." The anxiety in Cody's voice interrupted her thoughts.

Lisa's cell phone rang, and she dug through her purse, hoping to find it before it switched over to voice mail.

"I'll bet that's him. Can I answer it?"

"Sure, honey." Lisa's fingers finally connected with the phone. She scooped it from the bottom of her purse and held it out for her son.

Cody grabbed it and eagerly flipped it open. "Hey." He spoke quietly into the phone. "Yeah, OK."

Cody's chin trembled, indicating his disappointment. But his voice never hinted at it. She didn't need to hear the words to know exactly what Joe said to their son.

Lord, Joe's missing so much. Help him, please. Help him slow down and enjoy his son before it's too late. Cody will be grown and gone before he realizes it.

"I love you, too. See you tonight." Cody flipped the phone closed and handed it to Lisa, his eyes downcast. "Mr. Lee is making him work late. He won't be at the game."

His effort to rein in his emotions was a valiant one, and Lisa's heart went out to him. Hot anger tore through her. Her jaw tightened, and she fought to keep from clenching her teeth. Lucky for Joe, Cody had already hung up.

"Mom, please don't be mad at Dad. He has to work hard so he can pay for my birthday trip to Alaska next year. So we can go see the whales, remember?"

Lisa nodded, still trying to control her anger at Joe.

"Please say you won't be mad. Please? He's the best dad in the world."

How like Cody to forgive so easily. Why couldn't she do the same? Because it happened way too often, and she didn't like seeing her son repeatedly disappointed.

"I'll try, buddy. Come on. Let's go. We can't have you sitting on the bench."

"Hey, Mom, you're not paying attention," Cody complained a few minutes later as they headed down the winding road that made up Whidbey Island's highway. "I thought you wanted to sing the 'Cartoon Song.'"

"I do, honey. I'm sorry. I'm just—" Lisa shook her head. This situation was unfair to Cody. She shouldn't let her anger at Joe spoil his last baseball game. She glanced briefly at her son then quickly back at the road. He looked concerned, and she wanted to draw him into a hug but reached over and ruffled the top of his head instead.

"I'm just disappointed, honey. I wanted your dad to be there for your last game."

"I know, Mom. But it's Mr. Lee's fault, not his. And he said he'll show up if he can."

Yeah, right. Mike Lee would keep Joe until way

after Cody's bedtime if history was any indication. Joe worked so hard for the man, not only had he missed all of Cody's games, family dinners, and picnics in the park, he hadn't even been to church in months. Her anger sparked again, this time at Mike Lee.

But Cody shouldn't feel the obligation to play peacemaker between her, Joe, and Joe's boss. Not wanting to upset her son, she kept her opinion to herself. Lisa hit the gas a little harder than she should have as she pulled into the left-turn lane. Thankfully, the green arrow lit up just then, and she didn't need to hit the brake.

As she rounded into her turn, two things happened.

Cody burst into his mashed up version of the "Cartoon Song."

And Lisa realized with instant horror, the oncoming car failed to stop at the intersection.

With a mother's instinct, she threw her arm in front of Cody only to have it thrown against the dashboard when the other vehicle made impact with hers a split second later. The pain meant nothing to her, however, as she struggled against gravity to shield her son. She had to protect him, had to keep him safe.

"Cody! Cody!" She shouted his name repeatedly above the nightmarish sounds of skidding tires and crunching metal. "It'll be OK, honey. I promise."

Cody didn't answer. Desperate to touch her son, to reach out and comfort him, Lisa couldn't lift her arm no matter how hard she tried.

"Cody, stay awake for me, OK? Maybe we can sing the "Cartoon Song." Cody, can you hear me?"

Lisa struggled to stay conscious, afraid of closing her eyes, terrified she'd wake up to find her world changed forever. But her vision dimmed and blackness swirled around her. She mustered all the energy she could and whispered, "Cody, I love you so much, sweetheart."

Why didn't he answer? Desperate to hear his voice, frantic because she couldn't, Lisa strained to see him but the darkness continued to envelop her.

Please, Lord, take care of my little boy. Please, let him be OK.

Tears trailed down her face, but Lisa couldn't lift her hand to wipe them away.

"Lord, please," she whispered just before darkness claimed her, "don't take my son away from me."

1

Ten months later

The blinking light on the answering machine flickered, fast, furious, needy for attention. An unwelcome emotion tore at Joe Kendall's gut. *Ignore it. Just walk away.*

He should leave the room. Leave the voice mail unheard. Pretend he hadn't seen the annoying red light. Then the message wouldn't impact his heart. But he couldn't leave.

An inexplicable desperate need filled him, a need to hear the voice that would fill the room when he pressed the button.

Lisa. She called everyday like clockwork, and Joe found himself alternately looking forward to *and* dreading the calls.

The answering machine was a blessing. He didn't have to speak to her yet could listen to the sweet sound of her voice without her knowing how it affected him.

Easing behind the huge oak desk beneath the windows at the far end of his office, he settled into the chair of butter-plush leather—a gift from Lisa when he'd been offered a junior partnership in the firm.

Before he could push the button to listen to the message, someone rapped on the door. His boss, Mike Lee, walked into the room without waiting for a response.

"Joe, we need to talk."

"Hey, Mike. What's up?" He tried to sound pleasant, even though the interruption irritated him.

Mike rubbed his hand over the top of his short, thinning hair. Something was wrong. Not only did Mike not usually burst into his office, his head wasn't usually beet-red.

"It's the other senior partners." Mike sighed and rubbed his scalp again then sat in one of the chairs in front of Joe's desk. "Joe, there's no easy way to say this. A few of them are calling for your resignation."

"What?" Joe straightened in his chair. This couldn't be happening. "But I'm a partner."

"I know. That's why they've agreed to give you another chance."

Relieved, Joe let his shoulders relax. "Thank you," he whispered.

"Don't get too comfortable. There's a stipulation."

Joe tensed again.

"They want you to take a leave of absence. You have the rest of the week to get your cases cleared up or reassigned. After that, you're on a mandatory leave of absence."

"But—"

"Don't even try to talk your way around it. They won't consider anything less. It was the best I could do."

Joe rose from behind his desk and walked over to the window that faced Penn Cove. A few houses stood on the bluff across the water. One of those houses belonged to him and Lisa. If he lost his job, they'd lose the house. He couldn't let Lisa lose one more thing. He cleared his throat in order to hide his emotion. "For how long?"

"Two weeks."

Two weeks? Joe had no idea how to fill two weeks' worth of time. Not without work. It was the only thing that kept him going. Unsure what to say, he stared out the window. A boat with a faded red sail bobbed around in the choppy water.

"Joe, there's something else we need to talk about." Joe tensed at Mike's tone. "Friend to friend," Mike added quickly. "Why don't you sit back down?"

"I think I'll stand. Thanks." Joe continued to look out at the window.

"You should seriously consider filing for a divorce."

Joe turned around so fast he bumped into the potted fig and knocked several of the dry leaves loose. They fluttered to the ground and crunched into bits on the carpet beneath Joe's feet as he stepped toward Mike. "File for divorce? Are you for real?"

Mike stood and joined Joe at the window. He stared across the water as if looking at Joe and Lisa's house. "When was the last time you saw her?"

Joe blew out a heavy breath, not wanting to have this conversation. He clenched and unclenched his fists. "Don't, Mike," he warned in a low voice.

"Come on, Joe. I'm not trying to fight with you."

"It sure sounds like it. How would you like it if I made the same suggestion to you?"

"It's not the same thing. I go home to my wife every night." Mike stared at him, a challenge in his light blue eyes.

"Yeah, well, things are different for me, and you know it."

"What's it been? Three months?"

"Two," Joe answered, feeling ashamed. Why did

Mike have to bring up this subject? "It really isn't your business."

"I feel like it is. You're my friend. You're my co-worker. I just went to bat for you in a room full of men who want you gone. You owe me."

"And I'm supposed to repay you by divorcing my wife?"

"No. Not to repay me. To let her go. You haven't seen her in two months. Before that, you were always mentally absent. You're wallowing in guilt so heavy you can't even see what you're doing to her."

"I know what I'm doing to her," Joe snapped. "Do you think this is easy for me?" The guilt swallowed him a little more each day. He certainly didn't need any reminders from Mike.

"You need to find closure, Joe."

"Closure? I'm so sick of you throwing that word in my face. What I need is—" *My wife and my son.* "Get out, Mike. Go home to *your* wife."

Mike nodded and clapped him on the shoulder in what was probably meant to be a show of support. Joe shrugged Mike's hand off and turned back to the window. "I said get out."

"Fine. But think about it. Until you find a way to deal with your grief, you're no good for Lisa, and you're no good for yourself." Mike started out the door but stopped and turned back for one last parting shot. "If you truly love her, which I'm beginning to doubt, you'd let her get on with her life, Joe. Give her a chance to find a little bit of happiness."

Fists clenched, Joe started toward the door but stopped as Mike closed it behind him. He struggled for self-control. Fighting with Mike wasn't worth losing his job. Still, what did Mike know about it? Joe loved

Lisa more than anything. That's why he stayed away from her.

With a resigned sigh, he went back to his desk and pushed the button on the machine. Settling into his chair, he leaned back and listened.

"Hi, Joe. It's me." The soft gentle tones were Lisa's usual manner. Letting his eyes drift shut, he could picture her standing there, blue eyes sparkling with joy and excitement as they used to, her touch light on his arm.

"We haven't talked in a while." Her birthday. Two months almost to the day. He knew exactly how long it had been, just like he remembered every detail of his last-ditch effort to try and repair things.

"I know you're avoiding me, Joe. Please come home." If possible, her voice had softened even more. Lady-like, never demanding or whiny.

With a groan, he buried his face in his hands wishing he could go home, knowing he couldn't go there, couldn't face Lisa day after day, where he would be met with the hurt in her eyes—hurt he'd caused.

He'd hoped the specially planned birthday weekend would erase the deep sadness from her eyes. But it hadn't. If anything, it made things worse. For whatever reason, he didn't know. But he'd stayed away after that.

It was better this way, better for both of them.

"You have to be tired of sleeping in your office."

Though he'd never admit it to her or anyone else, he was. He had a persistent ache in his back and a crick in his neck from tossing and turning and trying to get comfortable on the small couch.

"Joe, I want you to take the trip."

The trip. Something deep in his gut froze, and his

heart began to pound. This wasn't the first time Lisa mentioned the trip. But this time he actually considered it.

"It would be good for you. Get away. Relax your mind and your soul. Maybe..." Joe could hear the hesitation in her voice and pictured her standing at the kitchen counter, phone pressed to her ear, staring out at the trees in the backyard. She would be watching for birds. She loved birds.

"Maybe it will help you deal with...you know...him." Her voice trailed off as if she couldn't bring herself to say his name. Just as Joe couldn't bear hearing it.

Cody. His son. *Their* son. Losing him altered his life in ways he'd never imagined possible. He couldn't imagine anything worse. Not even the breakdown of his marriage.

Something hot and unwelcome burned at the back of his eyes. He squeezed them tight and shook his head. Lisa actually believed going on a trip to Alaska, the trip originally intended as a family vacation for Cody's tenth birthday, would be good for him. Try as he might, he just didn't see how.

But right now he didn't have much choice. What else could he do? Unless he pulled himself together and found *closure,* he'd be out of a job. His law firm considered him a fast growing liability.

And once he cleared his desk and reassigned his cases, he'd have nowhere to stay. He'd been sleeping on the couch in the little den in his office. He could either go home to Lisa—not an option—or he could stay in a hotel for a couple of weeks then go back to work and say he'd found the oh-so-magical cure—*closure.*

The old Joe would never have considered lying. But this Joe would if lying were the only way he could return to work.

"I'm not saying you should forget Cody, or even that you shouldn't be sad. I'm sad, too." Joe heard the catch in Lisa's voice and pictured her face. The look he imagined broke his heart all over again.

"I'll probably be sad forever. So will you. But Joe, we should be doing this together."

No, he couldn't do it together. He didn't deserve to do anything with Lisa ever again. Heal, laugh, love. None of it.

Pain simultaneously tightened his throat and chest. He wished she would just forget about him. But she wouldn't. She was persistent, trying to wear him down. He was on the verge of giving in, and it scared him.

"Think about it, Joe."

Thinking hurt too much.

Being away from work, out there on a cruise ship, would give him too much opportunity to think. He didn't want to think. That's why he hid at work. He could forget about his personal life, lose himself in his cases. At least that's what he thought he'd been doing until Mike just set the record straight.

Joe found himself quickly coming to a decision he'd never imagined he'd make. This time instead of ignoring her message, he would answer it. But only because of this new situation Mike had forced on him.

If it would help Lisa in any way, he would do it. He would hide out on the cruise ship for a couple of weeks then go back to work and tell Mike the time away did him a lot of good. He'd do an exceptional job of convincing him. He had to. If he lost his job, he couldn't support Lisa. Losing her financial means was one more loss he wasn't willing to put her through.

He sighed in resignation then folded his arms on the desk and rested his head against them. He tried to take comfort in listening to Lisa on the answering machine.

"Joe?" Her voice softened even more, and Joe braced himself for what always came next.

"I love you." And then her final whispered plea. "Please, come home."

That was his cue to reach over and mute the answering machine before the mechanical voice could declare, "End of messages." He would rather Lisa's final words hang in the air, despite their effect on him.

Right now, he was especially vulnerable because she had the tickets in her possession and he'd have to call and ask for them. Somehow, he'd have to convince her to stay home. He certainly couldn't handle being cooped up with her for two weeks.

His hand trembled as he reached for the phone. Joe preferred to run away, hide—anything but talk to her. Conversing with her forced him to face the reality of the situation.

Their son, Cody, was gone. Forever. Never to be in their lives again.

Joe couldn't deal with the guilt.

****

The phone rang as Lisa started to pour a cup of hot water for her friend, Rose Gentry. After a quick glance at the caller ID, her hand trembled and she set the teakettle back on the stove.

"Lisa, it's me, Joe."

"I know." Not daring to hope what it might mean, she couldn't seem to raise her voice above whisper. It had been far too long since she'd heard his voice.

Hot tears burned the back of her eyes. Grateful to hear him now, she couldn't help but wish they could talk face-to-face. She'd take what she could get, though. Then a little whisper of fear brushed her heart. "Are you—is everything OK?"

"Yes." He hesitated just a bit. Then he cleared his throat. "Look, Lisa, I need to ask—do you still have the tickets for the cruise?"

Dare she even hope?

He spoke the words so fast she couldn't be entirely sure she heard correctly. Had Joe finally come around and realized what he'd been doing to himself? To her? To their marriage?

"Please, Lord," she whispered.

"What?"

He'd heard her. Now he'd know how desperate she was to have him back. No, not just to have him back. To have him snap out of this dark cloud of despair and start living again. Not that she had really started living again either. She missed her son as much as Joe did, and certainly considered herself equally— no *more*—guilty over his death.

"Nothing," she said quickly. "Yes, of course, I have the tickets."

"Good. I need them. You weren't planning on using them, were you?"

The truth hit her like a punch to the gut. He didn't want her to go with him.

"No." Somehow, she managed to speak through the painful constriction of her throat. Her heart broke all over again. Could he be taking someone else? No.

She knew Joe well enough. He might be hiding himself away from their marriage, but he would never cheat on her.

Slowly she sank onto the couch, cast Rose a woeful glance, and then shook her head. Rose gave Lisa a sympathetic look in return, with the emphasis on *pathetic,* which described Lisa to a T.

When would she quit hoping for Joe to come home?

Never.

To quit hoping would be to give up on Joe, and she'd never stop praying for him to cope with their loss. In the same way, she'd never stop praying for a chance to live that awful day over so she could do things differently. As long as she had breath, she would pray for those things.

Rose went over to the cupboard and rifled through an assortment of tea bags. She held up a black cherry one and waved it in Lisa's direction. Lisa nodded, and Rose filled the cup with steaming water.

"Lisa, I'm planning to take the cruise. But I really need to be alone. If you're sure you're not planning to go, I'll be by to get my ticket."

"Sure, Joe, of course. When do you want to come over? I'll make sure I'm here."

"That's just it, Lisa. I don't think we should see each other. Just leave the ticket on the porch under the planter, and I'll pick it up."

He didn't want to see her.

She thought back to that last weekend they'd spent together, her birthday, and swallowed hard. That weekend, she thought everything would be all right between them, but it wasn't. And his not wanting to see her was her reminder that it hadn't meant anything to him. She blinked back tears, not liking what his quick dismissal did to her heart.

"I'll put them in an envelope."

"Thanks." He was quiet, but she thought she heard a catch in his breath, as if he wanted to say something but changed his mind. Then she heard the soft click of the phone and knew he'd hung up.

"Bye, Joe," Lisa whispered anyway. She could have kicked herself for the watery sound in her voice. Having Rose as a witness made it even worse. Thank goodness, Joe hadn't heard it.

As they sipped their tea, Lisa relayed the conversation. Rose sat forward with interest and had just one thing to say. "Honey, you're going on that cruise."

2

Two Weeks Later

Saturday afternoon, Lisa and Rose stood on the sidewalk not far from the Seattle pier where the cruise ship *Northern Lights* rose out of the water and dwarfed everything in sight.

Nothing good ever came of lying.

Lisa looked up at the giant ship and gulped. It stood at least ten times the size of a Washington State ferry—until now, the largest boat she'd ever been on. Tiny lifeboats were placed at intervals across the side of the ship facing her. No doubt, the other side looked the same. Were there enough for the mass of people on the ship? Would they need them? An image from *Titanic* flashed through her mind, and her knees buckled.

"Easy," Rose said. "Are you all right?"

"I'm—I don't think I can do this." Her voice rose in pitch. She hated the way it sounded. Unsure. Insecure. Both were things she'd fought so hard to overcome.

This was crazy. She let her nerves take hold of her imagination and invent fear where there'd never been fear before. She raised one shoulder in a half-hearted gesture.

"Oh, no you don't." Rose pushed a button on her tiny remote, and the back door of her dark blue SUV slowly lifted. "You've come this far. You can't back out now. I won't let you." She gestured to the small suitcase and matching travel bag sitting neatly side-by-side.

"But it's all a big lie." They'd had this argument before, and no matter how Rose tried to justify it to Lisa, she still believed it was a mistruth. "And I've never lied to Joe before."

Unless she considered the biggest lie of all—not revealing her responsibility in the accident that took their son. He didn't know Lisa had charged through the intersection the instant her light turned green. Somehow, she'd never had the nerve to tell him. Nor had she told him about her friendship with Rose, whose husband had been driving the other car.

Rose sighed and rolled her dark brown eyes. "Is it really a lie? You told Joe you weren't planning to use the tickets." She shrugged. "So you changed your mind. No big deal."

Except it was a big deal. Lisa knew Joe wouldn't go on the cruise if he thought for a second she'd be there. Not telling him was a deception, and deception equaled lying. She said as much, but Rose still argued.

"Just remember he's your husband. You're doing this for him. It's for a noble purpose. Now come on, hon. You have a marriage to save."

For Rose to put so much effort into helping her with her marriage, when Rose herself no longer had one, touched Lisa so deeply tears misted her eyes.

"Thank you," Lisa whispered. She offered her friend a weak smile, not wanting to admit her nerves loomed as large as the ship. Then she slowly pulled the bags out of the SUV and set them on the curb. As she did, a thousand new doubts cluttered her mind. She stared at the festive-looking giant of a cruise ship, and every one of those doubts plunged toward her stomach.

No. She couldn't back out now. This was for Joe. He needed her, whether he knew it or not. She would go, albeit on shaky legs, for her husband. She had to help him find a way to deal with his grief over Cody without it further paralyzing his life. For him, she'd conquer every nerve in her body if it would help retrieve him from that very dark place where he'd retreated.

"I have to go," she whispered. "I have to."

"Yes, you do." Compassion darkened Rose's eyes and she leaned over to pull Lisa into a warm hug.

"It'll be OK, hon," Rose whispered when she finally let Lisa go. "It's all going to work out. You'll see."

Around them, people scrambled every which way. They looked happy and hopeful in spite of the overcast skies. Lisa envied them. Walking out of the house this morning, she'd also been hopeful. Now, her heart slammed in her chest, and her insides launched into a free-fall. The damp air brushed against her face, and she reached up to smooth her hair.

"I wish I could believe it, Rose. I'm so afraid lying will only make things worse."

"No." Rose shook her head. "I already told you. You aren't lying."

Lisa opened her mouth to protest, but Rose interrupted. "You changed your mind, nothing more. Didn't we just settle this?"

With your encouragement, Lisa wanted to say. But she didn't. Instead, she sighed. "We did. It's just nerves talking."

"OK." Rose smiled and nodded in understanding.

"But nerves or not, you're going. And that's final, because I'm not giving you a ride home. God wants you two back together."

"You'd better watch out. You're starting to sound like you believe." Though Lisa teased, deep down she hoped and prayed her friend would believe again.

Rose waved her hand as if swatting a pesky fly. "Not. Don't go getting your hopes up on my account."

While she might sound flippant, Lisa knew Rose used the tone to cover her true feelings. A soul-deep weariness haunted Rose's dark eyes. The last several months had been hard on both of them in such a similar way. No matter what happened in the future, the Lord stood firmly on Lisa's side. If Rose felt God's gentle tug, she didn't recognize it—at least not yet.

"It won't ever happen," Rose said. "Not unless God finds a way for Rob and RJ to walk back through the door."

Lisa's heart broke for the raw grief on her friend's face. Somehow, through the devastation, Lisa managed to hold on to her faith. Though it shamed her to admit, there were times when it was weaker than other moments, and the occasional doubt would creep in. Whenever her faith seemed to be on shaky ground, Lisa always managed to refocus on the Lord. Even if she didn't always *feel* His presence—a fact that troubled her greatly—she still *knew* He was there with her.

Even now, months later, Lisa woke up late at night, remembering. It always began with the ache in her arm. An ache no pain medication would touch. Then her heart would begin to pound so hard she feared it would burst through her chest. It would echo in her ears, along with the horrible squealing, crunching sounds of twisting metal and breaking glass—and, most haunting and horrific of all, Cody's silence.

Then there were the times the "Cartoon Song" rang repeatedly through her mind. Not the way it was intended for the radio, but Cody's version of the song. Oh, how she longed to see the grin on his face and hear his sweet, happy voice sing it one more time.

Legally, the accident wasn't Lisa's fault. Morally, and most definitely in her heart, Lisa was the one responsible. If she hadn't been in such an all-fired hurry to get Cody to his baseball game that day, if she hadn't been so angry at Joe for getting caught up in his work, as usual, and not getting home in time to go to the game with them, perhaps she would have been more cautious.

But even when ugly, noxious guilt ate away at Lisa, she forced herself to pray and keep her eyes focused on the Lord.

Sadly, Rose seemed unable to do the same. Lisa could only hope and pray her friend would someday open her eyes and realize their very friendship reflected a perfect example of God's presence in their lives. *Of His love.*

If anyone had told Lisa a few short months ago she would become a close friend of the woman whose husband caused the accident that killed her son, Lisa would have lashed out in anger. But the Lord had soothed her heart until the bitterness toward Rose melted away. Yes, the pain was still there. It would always be there. She hoped, though, that someday it would soften to a bruise.

At first, Lisa balked at what she knew were nudges from God, pushing her in Rose's direction. She wanted to nurse the hurt and bitterness. But through the Lord's gentle hand, she could see Rose was in pain as well. Not just with loss, for Rose had lost her son, too, along with her husband. No, Rose also ached with the pain of blame. She'd been arguing with her husband and believed he ran the red light because of the distraction. Her husband and son were dead, and Rose blamed herself.

Rose needed comfort and friendship as much as Lisa.

The miraculous result of their friendship amazed them both. Now Lisa loved Rose like a sister, and reaching out to Rose had helped ease some of Lisa's own pain.

Their friendship had been a huge step for both of them, and Lisa hoped Rose would eventually find her way back to the Lord. Unfortunately, Rose couldn't see past her feelings of guilt in order to step foot inside a church...let alone pray about it.

As they neared the pier, Rose pulled Lisa into a quick hug. "This is as far as I go. You're on your own from here." Then she whispered so softly Lisa barely heard her. "What am I going to do without you?"

"You'll be fine." Lisa noted the mist in Rose's big brown eyes.

"I'm being silly." Rose swiped at her tears.

"No, you're not." Lisa gave Rose a gentle smile. "Your friendship means the world to me, Rose. If Joe comes home, and I pray he does, nothing about our friendship will change. I promise."

"I don't know about that. Joe probably won't like you spending time with me."

Though she worried about the same thing, Lisa kept her thoughts to herself. "He doesn't pick my friends. Whether or not you want to believe it, our friendship is blessed by the Lord. In fact," she hesitated, wanting to say more but unsure of how Rose would receive her next words.

"What?"

Lisa pressed her lips together, took a deep breath, and silently prayed for guidance to say the right thing. "We've had a guest speaker at church for the last few weeks, doing a special series on friendship. It concludes tomorrow at the Sunday service."

The expression on Rose's face hardened, and Lisa feared she might have pushed too far.

"Don't worry," Lisa added quickly. "I wasn't going to suggest you go."

"Good." Rose visibly relaxed. "Because you know I won't."

"They're recording the series of lessons. If you'd like, when I get back, we can listen to them together, and you'll be able to see the same thing I do. God brought us together for a reason, Rose. Friendship, true friendship, comes from Him, and I'm blessed to have you in my life." Lisa meant what she said, and now it was her turn to grow misty-eyed.

Rose gave her another impromptu hug. "OK, now. You'd better get going or they'll sail without you."

Lisa's heart started to pound with dread. She tried to smile at her friend, but the muscles in her jaw remained tightly clenched.

"Everything will be fine; you'll see. When I come pick you up, you and Joe will walk toward me hand-in-hand."

Tears pricked Lisa's eyes again. She hoped like anything it would turn out just that way. But given how Joe had distanced himself from her, she sincerely doubted it. This whole thing seemed impossible, and she wished she'd never let Rose talk her into this.

Lisa knew Rose felt guilty not only for the accident, but also for the breakdown of Lisa and Joe's marriage. That's why she worked so hard to get the two of them back together, and why she tried so hard to convince Lisa taking this trip did not equal lying to Joe.

"I don't know, Rose. I just—it's just—it's not like he's going to fall into my arms or anything."

"No, but two weeks at sea in the same room…he won't be able to hide from you. Eventually he'll have to open up and talk. When he does, well, things will work themselves out. I know it."

"I hope you're right." Lisa wished she could be as positive as Rose.

"I am. Now get up that ramp and go save your marriage."

If only it could be so simple. Despite her doubts, Lisa hugged her friend one last time then turned to face what she prayed wouldn't end up being a disaster.

As she grabbed the handle of her luggage and headed up the steep ramp, people were everywhere. She could almost feel their buzz of excitement. Was Joe among them, smiling? *No.* He didn't smile anymore.

"Please, Lord, let this be the right thing."

Hope and dread mixed together as each footstep brought her closer to boarding the cruise ship, closer to Joe, and closer to the future.

Was Rose right? Did God want the two of them back together?

Yes, of course He did. God approved of marriage. He wanted to bless marriages. Why should hers be any different?

****

"What's the matter, buddy? You change your mind about the cruise?"

Joe tore his gaze from the window of the cab, only then realizing he'd been staring into nothingness.

His cab driver leaned over the back of the seat, watching him intently with inquisitive brown eyes.

Joe glanced away and stared out the window again, this time taking note of the large white cruise ship with dozens of brightly colored triangular flags strung from one end to the other.

In the distance, another ship blew its horn, gulls hollered, and people scurried every which way along the sidewalk—most struggling with luggage and heading toward the terminal. Many were family and friends sending their loved ones off with a merry farewell.

Family. Friends. The thought left him hollow, empty. *Lisa...Cody...*

"No, I haven't," he finally replied with a sick feeling in his gut, fully aware his tone belied his words.

"Humph." The driver nodded. Joe hadn't fooled him a bit, but Joe offered no explanation. There was no reason to burden this kind, friendly stranger with troubles of Joe's own making.

Relieved the driver hadn't asked if Joe was meeting someone, he paid the fare. Grabbing his luggage—a simple duffel bag—Joe headed slowly toward the terminal.

Check-in at the terminal proved uncomfortable and hectic. The clerk kept asking if Mrs. Kendall was already checked in and seemed confused when Joe twice responded he was traveling alone. Finally, she nodded out of sheer frustration then gave him directions and a swipe-card for his room.

"Oh, sir, your bag," She called after him. "We'll take it to your room for you while you enjoy the festivities on the Stargazer Deck."

"No festivities for me," Joe said. "I'm going straight to my room."

"But, sir," she called after him.

Joe didn't want to be rude, but neither did he want to engage in any kind of conversation where the other party tried to talk him into something. So he kept walking straight through the gate and up the blue steel ramp, until he stood on the main deck of the *Northern Lights*. People and noise surrounded him, annoying him, and doing absolutely nothing to calm his growing apprehension.

Trying to ignore the chaos, Joe managed to make his way to the Denali Deck. At the door to his room, he hesitated. Apprehension, even more fierce than before, gripped him.

Why was he here? Suddenly he didn't know, and it scared him. Did Mike really think this time away would fix all Joe's problems? Did Lisa really think this cruise would help him deal with the loss of Cody? Without a doubt, he'd feel this pain every day for the rest of his life.

And Lisa...Joe swallowed hard. Not hearing her voice on his answering machine every day for two weeks would be hard. Even though he wasn't supposed to look forward to it, even though he was supposed to close his heart to it, he couldn't help it. He shut off the wave of longing that threatened to overwhelm him. He couldn't allow himself to feel anymore. Especially now. He had to stay strong so he could follow through with his decision. Those daily messages from Lisa would stop once he returned and she learned of his plans.

As soon as he returned from this trip, he planned to follow through on Mike's suggestion and do the one thing he swore he never would. Something he didn't want, but something for Lisa's own good. He planned to file for divorce.

Divorce.

The hateful word stopped him cold because the reality of it was far worse than the word itself. It made him physically ill. No matter that it was the way he earned a living. He never encouraged anyone to take that step. In fact, much to his boss's chagrin, he often tried to talk clients out of a divorce and into marriage counseling. He and Lisa vowed they'd never let it happen to them. They'd been so naïve back then, so certain their love was strong enough to withstand anything. But then everything changed.

If only they could go back to the days of pain-free innocence.

After what happened to Cody, Joe would never be the same again. Neither would Lisa. And their marriage…it simply couldn't survive.

He should feel relieved to have come to the realization—no thanks to Mike's input—but the reality of it cut his heart to shreds. It was the best thing he could do for Lisa. His wife. Soon to be ex-wife. The woman he would love forever.

Joe opened the door to the room. There must have been a mistake. The room was the size of a small bedroom and couldn't be the family suite they'd booked. Someone somewhere messed up. Not that it really mattered now.

In a twist of irony, there were a set of bunk beds bolted to the wall. Cody would have enjoyed this far better than the family suite.

Another reminder of his son's enthusiasm. Another grip of pain—no less than he deserved.

Joe dropped his bag inside the entryway and shut the door. The sound of silence greeted him, and he looked around the room.

What should he do now? Sitting and staring would do nothing to help ease the pain and loneliness. He slumped down on the bottom bunk and closed his eyes. For once, he wished he could be like his boss and drown his sorrows in alcohol. He was a hopeless coward, running away: first from his son's death, then from his marriage, and now from the purpose of this trip.

Lulled by the gentle sway of the ship, Joe could imagine the water lapping at the side. What should be a feeling of comfort was one of torment. He didn't want to make this cruise without either of the two people who meant the world to him.

Cody. His son. The precious child he'd let slip away.

Lisa. His wife. A woman he'd turned his back on when she'd needed him the most.

As he drifted into a restless sleep, he thought of Lisa and wished like crazy she could be here with him. "I'm so sorry, Lisa," he whispered. He'd ruined everything. If only he could go back and change things. Make them like they were before.

Rolling over on to his side, Joe choked back a sob. Some things couldn't be fixed.

****

With a sigh, Lisa shifted her weight from foot to foot in an attempt to keep warm. Since boarding, she'd stood out in the cold on the sandpaper-rough surface of the cruise ship watching for Joe. It had really only been twenty minutes since she'd said good-bye to Rose, but twenty minutes was a long time to stand outside on a typical May morning in the Pacific Northwest.

A bitter gust of salt air whipped against her, prickling her nose and stinging her eyes. Still, it wasn't enough to make Lisa lift her chin out of her hands and pull away from the cold metal railing where her elbows were propped.

Chilled to the bone, she continued to watch as cars, cabs, and buses pulled up and enthusiastic passengers hopped out. Her husband was nowhere in sight. Perhaps she'd missed him. Or perhaps he'd boarded before she arrived and he'd already settled into his room.

Common sense told her to get out of the cold and find their room, but she couldn't take the chance of him seeing her before the ship set sail. Again, a jab of guilt rattled her.

Just then, she caught sight of a couple with a little boy tucked between them. The trio walked hand-in-hand up the ramp.

That should be her and Joe...and Cody.

Wishful thoughts. They'd never have Cody again, but they could have each other. If Joe would just let down his guard and open up to her; if he'd lean on her the way she always leaned on him. If he would simply open his heart and arms to her once more, they could have a life again. It wouldn't be the same life, but they would have each other. They would be together.

Life without Cody was barely tolerable. Not having Joe to share the pain with made it even more difficult. Did Joe ever reach out to the Lord for comfort and strength? She asked herself the same question every day over the last ten months, hoping and praying he did.

Be with him, Lord. Give him what he needs. She prayed he hadn't lost his faith as Rose had done. Maybe Lisa could help him find his way back.

To the Lord or to you? The stray thought caught her off-guard. To both, of course.

And if you can't help him? If he doesn't come back, what then?

Lisa tried to ignore the disturbing thought. Of course she could help Joe, but she didn't think for one minute it would happen right away. A loving wife was the last person he'd want to see. Her emotions were the last thing he'd want to deal with. And as much as she wanted his dark brown eyes to light up when he saw her, the way they used to, she knew it wouldn't happen.

Maybe Rose was wrong. Maybe this wasn't such a good idea after all.

Yes, it was. It had to be. This cruise was about Joe, about getting him back and healing him. No way would she give up now. Their marriage simply *had* to be saved, so Joe could step back into the real world and live again. Failure wasn't an option.

3

Though Lisa eventually gave up watching for Joe, she waited until the ship was well underway before she went to look for their room. *His* room, she reminded herself. At least now he couldn't send her away. On the other hand, neither could she change her mind and turn back.

Once out of the cold, Lisa pulled a small compact mirror from her bag and inspected herself with dismay.

The misty Northwest air had taken its toll and her short blonde curls sprang in every direction. She fiddled with it to no avail and finally puffed out a sigh. She could do nothing more.

Yes, she wanted to look her best, but it really wouldn't matter to Joe. She tucked the compact into the front pouch of her floral mini backpack and sighed again.

Even if she looked cover-model perfect, Joe would probably still take one look at her and run screaming into the night. Her heart fluttered, and she willed the sudden butterflies in her stomach to quiet down.

Now was not the time to lose her nerve. Too much hinged on this, and she hadn't waited all that time in the cold for nothing. She had to reach down into the very core of her being to re-light the spark of determination that brought her here to 608 Denali Deck and the door standing between her and Joe.

Holding her breath, Lisa inserted the key with a shaky hand.

An alarm sounded as she pulled the card from the slot. Startled, she jumped back, waiting for someone to tell her she had the wrong room. People scrambled out of their rooms as someone from the ship's crew began yelling.

"This is a drill, folks, just a drill. Please, report to your emergency muster sites. Hurry along, now."

Don't panic. Just breathe. Everything will be fine. Lisa took a breath and tried to think. If she reported to the muster site, Joe would see her. She wasn't ready to see him yet.

When she'd come off the elevator, she'd noticed a ladies' room. She watched while the man yelling instructions turned to answer questions from an elderly couple. While his back was turned, she raced down the corridor and ducked into the restroom. Hopefully no one would come searching for passengers, and she could wait there until the drill ended.

****

It seemed to Joe he'd just begun to drift into a restful asleep when the blast of alarms and sirens startled him. He bolted upright, hitting his head on the bunk above him.

A sharp rap on the door was followed by a young man's voice. "Emergency muster drill. Please report to your muster site."

Could nothing be easy? He wanted to be left alone. When the clerk at check-in mentioned the mandatory drill the cruise line had at the beginning of each cruise, he'd hoped it would be quiet and quick, and he could skip it without being noticed. Maybe even possibly sleep through it. No such luck apparently.

With a groan, Joe searched the floor for his shoes then pulled them on.

Just as he reached the door, a knock came again. He opened it to find a fresh-faced steward in a crisp, white uniform.

"Sir, the muster is mandatory." He spoke loud enough to compete with the alarms. "You and your wife need to report to the muster site right away."

"I'm on my way, thanks." Joe tried to be as polite as possible while shouting to be heard. It wasn't this young man's fault his life was falling apart. "But my wife isn't here."

A crease wrinkled the steward's forehead as he consulted the clipboard in front of him.

"Joseph Kendall?"

"Yes."

"This says Joseph and Lisa Kendall."

Stepping away from the doorway, Joe gestured for the steward to come in. "I can assure you I'm alone."

"Sorry, sir." The young steward crossed the threshold. "It's not that I don't believe you, but we're under strict orders to check all rooms to make sure everyone attends the drill."

"I understand." Joe shut the door, hoping to drown out some of the shrillness.

"And this," the steward tapped the clipboard, "says Mrs. Kendall has checked in."

"There was some confusion when I checked in, too. But I promise you, I'm alone." Joe followed him as he opened the first closet then the bathroom door. "If you contact the terminal, they'll tell you the same thing."

"It's OK, sir. I believe you."

But Joe could tell by the man's tone and body language, he didn't.

"Please follow me to the muster site." The steward stepped to the side to let Joe pass through the door first as if to make sure he didn't try to escape.

When he opened the door, Joe winced as the alarms pierced his ears all over again. But he did as instructed, thinking of Lisa every step of the way. This continuous mention of her made it seem like God conspired to keep her at the forefront of his mind.

Joe just wanted to push her from his thoughts.

Throughout the demonstration by the ship's crew on how to use the floatation devices, Joe remained distracted. If someone asked him to demonstrate what he'd just learned about the lifeboats, he would fail.

Images of Lisa nagged at him. Lisa, Cody, and the precious moments he'd let slip away while he built and maintained his law career.

When the drill ended and the sirens stopped wailing, there was no blessed silence for Joe. Instead, unwelcome memories raced through his mind as he headed back to his room feeling even lonelier than he had before.

****

Long after the drill ended, Lisa left the plush chair in the comfortable lounge of the ladies' room and headed toward Joe's room. Heart pounding, she twisted the door handle and prepared to greet her husband *and* their future.

As she opened the door, her breath escaped in a

whoosh. This definitely couldn't be right.

Standing on the threshold of the ship's room where she fully intended to spend the next two weeks saving her marriage, Lisa stared in disbelief. Bunk beds. Two twin beds bolted to the wall, one directly on top of the other. Yet this was obviously the right room because directly in front of her, his back to her, Joe sprawled out on the bottom bunk wearing a pale yellow polo shirt and faded blue jeans.

Just the sight of him warmed her heart, and she forgot her distress over the room. Hot tears stung the back of her eyes. It had been far too long since she'd seen her husband. She wanted to run to him, gather him in her arms, but he wouldn't welcome it.

Lisa plopped down in the olive green chair at the foot of Joe's bed and looked around the room with a gnawing feeling in the pit of her stomach. This was so *not* the luxurious stateroom they'd booked all those months ago.

This tiny, cramped room with a dime-sized porthole so high Lisa would have to stand on her tiptoes just to see her expensive ocean view...this couldn't be what they'd paid for.

A second olive chair sat under a tiny round table near the little porthole. A vanity stood bolted to the wall near the bottom bunk, next to a closet that looked like it might hold most of the clothes she'd brought. She was tempted to open it to see how the porter managed to squeeze her suitcase into it, but she didn't want to wake Joe.

Behind her, a door led to the bathroom. At least, she hoped it was the bathroom.

Where were the huge picture window and private balcony with cushy patio furniture she'd seen in the brochure at the travel agency? The kitchenette, the sitting room with the day bed, and the queen-sized bed were also missing.

Clearly, they'd been scammed by the travel agency. Especially considering this room should have originally been occupied by three people.

Her surroundings were nothing even remotely romantic. Not that romance was her main goal, of course. It wasn't even a secondary goal. Saving Joe was the main goal. Joe and his heart and soul. Romance, if it ever returned, would be an added bonus.

Feeling suddenly sad and claustrophobic, Lisa bit back tears of disappointment. She'd just have to make the best of it.

Her marriage depended on it.

As quietly as possible, she tiptoed to the bathroom. The longer Joe slept, the more time she had to repair the damage to her hair. *And* the more time she had to come up with the right words to say when he did wake up. Words to explain exactly why she'd come and why she intended to stay.

It wouldn't go over well, that much she knew. Joe had been running from her, his feelings, and their marriage since Cody's death. But the time for running was past.

Inside the small bathroom, Lisa made herself look as presentable as possible then slipped back into the room. She sat in the chair near Joe's bed and waited. He tossed and turned in his sleep and each time he moved, her heart pounded in anticipation of his reaction when he woke and found her there.

Not quite ready for the confrontation she knew would occur, Lisa could no longer quell the butterflies in her stomach.

In all his tossing and turning, Joe moved so his back faced the wall. The unsettled look on his face ripped at her heart. His dark brown hair fell across his forehead in unruly waves. Fine lines that weren't there a few short months ago now fanned the corners of his eyes. His lips pressed tightly together. She remembered a time when his soft, generous mouth always smiled, and his dark brown eyes were warm and inviting. Even during the years when she hadn't yet realized her marriage wasn't what it should be, Joe never failed to light up a room with his presence.

He may be able to run from his pain during his waking hours but, obviously, he couldn't escape it while he slept. Her husband was a tortured soul, and she ached to give him comfort.

"Joe," she whispered before reaching out to smooth his forehead. She stopped just before she actually touched him, let her hand hover for an indecisive moment, then settled for simply watching him toss and turn. Touching him would do nothing to ease his pain. It would only wake him, and she still needed a few more minutes to refocus her thoughts and gather the resolve that brought her here in the first place.

Afraid that if he stirred again she would grab on to him and never let go, Lisa rose and walked to the little window. Standing on her tiptoes, she stared out at the gray-green chop. White froth churned the angry saltwater, yet a strong sense of peace slowly settled deep in her being.

Yes, she needed to be here.

Here, with Joe.

Here to repair her husband's heart and, hopefully, with help from the Lord, their marriage.

4

Joe awoke feeling hollow and thinking about Lisa. So much so, he could imagine the light citrusy fragrance he'd come to associate as a part of her.

Wishful thinking. He kept his eyes closed, not wanting anything to detract from the image of her in his mind. Even though he didn't want to admit it to himself, Lisa's presence would be something of a comfort. But she wasn't here, and he needed to accept it. Not her choice, of course, but his. He chose to be alone. She didn't deserve this painful limbo he inflicted on her, and he didn't deserve comfort.

Trying to find a position that would let him fall back asleep so he could avoid thinking about things he couldn't fix, Joe tossed and turned again. The movement of air carried the unmistakable scent of citrus. He inhaled deeply. That scent was real and so very familiar it hurt to even breathe. It had to be an air freshener of some kind, something they used here on the cruise ship. Otherwise, he missed Lisa far more than he could even admit to himself.

Before he'd come fully awake, he'd been dreaming of her…and Cody…and all he'd lost, all he'd run from. He lay there for a minute trying to content himself with the gentle movement of the ship, hoping it would somehow give him a sense of peace and lull away his thoughts of them.

"It's my fault," he whispered through a throat

tight with emotion. He groaned as a fresh wave of pain cut his heart. "I did this to us. My fault."

"No, Joe. Stop blaming yourself."

Startled, Joe opened his eyes and stared into Lisa's wide blue ones.

Lisa? He blinked. Surely, he imagined she knelt next to him, worry lining her small face.

He even reached out to touch her, certain she'd fade away the instant his hand came near.

Flesh contacted flesh at the same moment her pupils widened, and she sucked in a breath.

He sat up with a jerk.

She stood and stepped back.

This was no dream. Lisa. Here, for real, right where he needed her *not* to be.

Now that he'd reached a decision about the divorce, the last thing he needed was to deal with her emotions. Not until he could deal with his own.

"Lisa?" He kept his tone steady, even, careful to keep any hint of disconcertedness from his voice. He didn't want her to know how her presence shook him.

Brushing her blonde bangs away from her eyes, she knelt down beside him again. Her eyes were bright with unshed tears, and the gentle curve of Lisa's lips held an almost undetectable tremor as she searched his eyes with her own. There was something in her expression he couldn't quite pinpoint, but he knew her well enough to know she was trying to be strong for him instead of herself.

He'd let her down. That wounded look in her eyes could be attributed to no one but him. Not Lisa herself for being angry with him right before the accident. And not Rob Gentry, even though he'd run the red light at the intersection.

"Why didn't you tell me you were coming?"

"Because then you would have refused to come. You forget I know you, Joe. I know you thought you could shut yourself up in this room thinking it would all go away."

He looked down and away from her gaze. "If I didn't know you so well, I'd think you planned it this way." Embarrassed, uncomfortable that she knew him so well, Joe's voice came out sharper than intended.

He turned away from her so he wouldn't accidentally look up and see the hurt in her eyes. Unbelievable. His sweet, quiet wife had flat out blindsided him.

"I guess I should say I'm sorry. I didn't intend to come, but I—I did change my mind."

Lisa's soft apology tore at his gut. How should he respond? To tell her not to worry about it would be like saying he didn't mind her being here. Which he did. But to say so would only shovel more hurt onto her already broken heart.

"I guess I just don't understand why you changed your mind." He tried to gentle his tone so as not to hurt her any further.

"I need to say good-bye, too. I—" She bit down on her lip and looked away. Joe could see tears welling in her eyes as she fought for control. A lump the size of his fist rose in his throat, and he couldn't seem to swallow past it.

"I think I hoped if I went on the cruise, saw the things Cody had looked forward to seeing, maybe—I don't know." She shook her head, and Joe could see her struggle to maintain her composure. He wanted to take her in his arms. Somehow, he resisted.

"I guess I just wanted it to help."

"And now?"

"I don't know. Just like you need to be here, Joe, so do I. I'll stay out of your way. I promise."

Impossible. Just being in the same room with her—He'd never survive this trip without losing his resolve. And yet, she was here. They'd left the dock. He couldn't very well throw her overboard.

"Joe, I promise I won't bug you. You go your way, and I'll go mine. I just need to get away, too. I didn't realize it until the other day. Rose and I were talking and—"

"Rose? Rose Gentry?"

Lisa looked away from him and walked toward one of the chairs. To distance herself from him because talking to Rose might hurt him? Or because she'd merely mentioned the woman's name?

As she sat in the chair, Joe noticed how much weight she'd lost. The last time he saw her, Lisa couldn't afford to lose even a mere five pounds. Clearly, she'd lost a good deal more because her clothes were way too baggy. He started to say something but held back.

Finally, she looked at him, her blue eyes shaded with nervousness and something else he didn't recognize.

"She's my friend, Joe. I don't mean to hurt you with that, but she needs someone." Her voice wavered for only a brief moment before it strengthened with challenge. "She's all alone, just like me. Just like you. Like it or not, I can't turn my back on her."

Lisa clenched and unclenched her hands then looked down at her lap. Clearly, she thought her friendship with Rose upset him. It didn't. Quite the opposite. It reminded him of his own shame; shame at forgetting that Rose also lost a major portion of her life—her husband and son. At least Lisa had the decency to approach the woman and give her the comfort she needed, while he was just a coward who ran from everything. Lisa's taking the time to befriend Rose warmed a tiny piece of his heart.

Something else gave him pause. Something Joe barely wanted to admit to himself. A part of him couldn't help but wonder…if Lisa could forgive Rose, could she find it in her heart to forgive him? Lisa's nature would never let her show she blamed him. She might never even admit it to herself, but deep down she had to blame him as much as he blamed himself. He couldn't, nor should he ever, expect Lisa to forgive him. They were finished. Totally. The sooner he accepted it the better, because he had a daunting task ahead of him—getting her to accept it as well.

"It's all right, Lisa. Despite the way I've treated you, I'm not a monster. You can say Rose's name without worrying about my reaction. I don't blame her."

When she looked up at him, her eyes were wide. Because he said he wasn't a monster? Or maybe because he didn't blame Rose.

Or maybe, and possibly worse, she recognized his acknowledgment of his treatment toward her. He cringed. "I only blame myself."

"No, Joe." She stood and walked toward him, and he held up his hand. Much as he wanted to reach out and hold her, he couldn't. If he did, he'd be lost, never able to let her go. And she'd end up hurting a lot worse than this. "Don't try to comfort me, Lisa."

"But—"

"I said *don't*. In fact, it would be better if you just

leave."

"No."

"Lisa—"

"I'm not leaving," she interrupted in a surprisingly obstinate tone.

Was that what he'd seen in her eyes earlier and hadn't recognized? Stubborn determination? One to avoid confrontation, Lisa was always the first to back down. But not this time, apparently. "Lisa, I really can't deal with this right now. I don't want you here." He tried his best to sound intimidating, certain she'd turn around and slip through the door. But he knew he simply sounded weary.

Lisa didn't back away. She just stood there, hands on slender hips, fire blazing in her blue eyes. "I'm not leaving," she repeated.

"I really need to be alone. Given what we've both been through, I'd think you'd understand." If appealing to her emotions meant playing dirty, so be it. He had to get her out of here. Two weeks sharing a room with the woman he loved but intended to divorce—torture. *Emotional* torture. And how could he even begin to get a handle on his life so he could return to work?

"And exactly where do you expect me to go?" Her response held no indication of being intimidated or of changing her mind—though she did sound sad. He looked closely. Were those tears hovering below the surface of her blue eyes? He couldn't let it matter.

"You could get off in Vancouver."

Her eyes widened for a split second. Clearly, she didn't realize the ship would dock in British Columbia early in the evening to pick up the Canadian crew. He knew only because he'd overheard someone talking about it in the elevator.

"Absolutely not, Joe." She steeled her expression into one of fierce determination. It matched her tone of voice. "I'm taking this cruise, too. It was meant as a family vacation, and we're taking it together even if we aren't a family anymore."

Those words got to him. Whether she meant them to or not, they hurt. They weren't a family anymore; they'd never be a family again, and she had no business here.

"The only way I'm getting off in Vancouver is if you physically throw me off."

It was a dare, but one he wouldn't take. Joe had never lifted a finger against her, and he never would.

"Then we'll find you another room, because you're not staying with me."

"It's not like we have money to throw around. This trip cost enough as it is, and what did we get for our money?" She waved her arms dramatically, pointing out the shortcomings of the room. "There are two beds. It's not like you'll have to share more than the room with me."

How could he make her understand? He needed to be alone. Desperation had him raising his voice louder. "This is *my* room, Lisa, where *I* came to be alone. So I could say good-bye to my son. Something I didn't want to do, but something I was forced into."

Her mouth dropped open, and she stepped closer. "Listen here, Joseph Kendall. I had nothing to do with Mike's decision."

No, but she obviously knew about it. He hadn't told her. He merely said he decided to take the cruise. So who had? Mike? It couldn't have been anyone else. His respect for his boss just dropped another notch.

Add lack of confidentiality to the list of reasons to begin the search for another job when he returned home.

"I'm not going anywhere. It's ridiculous to waste money on another room when this one's perfectly fine. If you're uncomfortable with me being here, find a way to deal with it." A splash of pink brightened both cheeks, and Lisa stood firm, authoritative. He almost expected her to reach out and poke him in the chest. When had she turned so assertive?

"You aren't the only one in pain here." Lisa plunked back down on the chair, folded her arms, and glared at him. "Cody was my son, too. Like it or not, you're stuck with me for the next two weeks."

Stunned, Joe could only stare at his wife. Shy, and often unsure of herself when faced with even the mildest of confrontations, Lisa always spoke softly and seemed timid. Her timidity attracted him in the beginning but drove him away in the end.

Not that Joe was being confrontational now, but he did his best to convey he wanted to be alone. Yet Lisa showed no sign of giving in. Sometime in the last few months she'd found the ability to speak up in defense of herself. Clearly, Rose's friendship was good for Lisa.

"You *need* to grieve for Cody, Joe. But locking yourself away from the world isn't the way. This cruise isn't for you to hide yourself away like this, like you've done for the past several months."

Her words gave him pause. *Hide away*. That's exactly what he planned to do, exactly what he needed. Perhaps if he'd done something like this sooner, they wouldn't be in this situation now. Of course, there wasn't room for second-guessing. As sad as it made him feel, it was too late to go back now.

She glared at him, determined.

Again, the painful awareness that the breakdown of their marriage was his fault struck him. "I can't do this, Lisa. I can't—"

"What? Deal with me? With your emotions? It's the reason I'm here. To help you. I'm your wife."

"I don't want or need your help. I want and need to be alone."

"I can't let you."

"Do what you want then." Joe headed toward the door. "If you won't leave, I will." He stormed out of the room and into the hall, wishing like anything he could forget the look of shock and grief on Lisa's face.

Together only a few minutes, and he'd hurt her all over again. *Good going, Joe.* He slapped the heel of his hands into his forehead.

****

The slamming of the door echoed painfully loud in her ears. Lisa resisted the urge to go after Joe but knew it would do no good. He'd made up his mind. The determination had sparked in his eyes. She prayed he wouldn't get off the ship in Vancouver.

Oh, Joe, you are in such trouble.

She'd made a horrible mistake in coming here. Joe *needed* to be here, and she'd scared him off.

He so obviously needed to find peace. More than the rescue of their marriage, Joe's relationship with God needed to be salvaged. Lisa couldn't believe she'd put her own needs above Joe's. Rose would say she didn't, that she wasn't being selfish. But Lisa knew better.

Even though she'd voiced to herself that Joe's

needs were more important than their marriage, she'd remained focused on getting Joe to come home. She'd made it her number one priority. She could justify it a hundred different ways, but the bottom line remained. She'd had it all backward.

As Lisa's mind touched on that one thing, it rocked her with a soul-jarring clarity. She'd known it all along on some level, but selfishness pushed her own wants and needs to the forefront of her mind. She wanted Joe back, needed him back. But he needed something more, something above all else. *The Lord. God.* Joe had grown so far from his Savior; his relationship with the Father needed mending. More than their marriage being saved, Joe needed a renewal of faith.

Why hadn't she seen it sooner? Because she'd been so consumed with her own needs. She'd figured if her marriage was secure that she could help Joe find his way back to the Lord. But in reality, Joe's soul was the most important, and if he found his way back to the Lord, their marriage might possibly be saved. But if not…at least Joe's soul could rest.

With a trembling hand, Lisa swiped at her tears. It wasn't as if her motives were evil.

Could it be so wrong to want to help her husband deal with his grief, to want to help him find peace? Those pain-laced words he'd uttered upon waking tore at her heart. He'd sounded so lost…looked so lost. The pain darkening his eyes was so immediate it took her breath away.

Joe blamed himself for the accident even though he'd never come right out and say it. She'd suspected it was the reason he'd retreated further into himself until finally he'd quit coming home at all. She knew he slept on the couch in his office. His law firm was in a building that housed a large fitness center, so he probably showered there. Where he washed his laundry, where he ate his meals, she could only guess.

Oh, Joe. What has happened to us?

Comfort. Joe badly needed it. She did, too. But given the tormented words he'd spoken earlier, he needed it more. As his wife, Lisa should be the one to give it to him. But so far, she'd failed.

****

Long after they departed Vancouver, Joe sat at a table in the observation section on the Stargazer Deck.

The dark chilly night made it the perfect environment to be alone. It matched his mood. The occasional couple strolled by, but they afforded him barely a glance before they shared kisses in the moonlight or marveled over the sight of the now distant and fading Vancouver skyline.

He'd almost disembarked in Vancouver. Something stopped him, though he couldn't say what. Most likely because *they*—Lisa, his boss, his co-workers—were right. Much as he hated to admit it, getting away would be good for him. And if he happened to find the closure they kept spouting about, so much the better. Even though he wasn't convinced he deserved it, he supposed deep down he really wanted it.

Yes, that's probably why he'd stayed on board. It certainly couldn't be because of Lisa's presence.

Unfortunately, he'd have to face her sooner or later. With a fully booked ship, he had nowhere to go except his own room unless he wanted to sit out here all night. He didn't. He'd almost be willing to, just to make a point, but then he could hardly stay outside for the entire two weeks. And the closer they got to Alaska, the more he risked turning into a freezer-pop just to make a point to Lisa. And that would be foolish since he didn't really know what point he wanted to make.

Much to his relief, Lisa appeared to be asleep in the top bunk when he let himself into the room.

Hours later, as he lay in the dark listening to the soft sound of her breathing, Joe wished he could fall asleep as well. Occasionally, he detected a hint of her citrusy fragrance. It did things to his heart. Things he didn't understand, things he sure didn't want to contemplate.

Once again, he had to ask himself the question: how on earth could he share this tiny room with her for the next two weeks?

5

Early the next morning, Lisa was relieved to find
Joe sleeping in the bunk below her. After checking
several times during the night to see if he had come
back to the room, she'd finally fallen asleep certain
he'd gotten off the ship in Vancouver. She'd climbed
up and down the ladder of the bunk bed so many
times, her legs ached this morning.

Now, staring at Joe, she blinked back unexpected
tears. He appeared to sleep fitfully, without any hint of
peace. She resisted the urge to reach out and comfort
him. Instead, she quietly gathered her things for a
shower.

When she came out of the bathroom, he was still
asleep. Too edgy to sit around the room waiting for
another confrontation with him and certain there
would be one as soon as he woke, Lisa decided to
explore the ship.

Her first impression of the liner being huge was
right on the mark. A floating city, Lisa never imagined
it could be so large. Besides what must be hundreds of
people, there was an amazing number of restaurants,
cafés, lounges, and gift shops.

As she walked past one of the gift shops, a vase of
tulips in the window caught her eye. Tulips reminded
her of Joe. She hoped they, in turn, reminded him of
her.

On impulse, Lisa entered the shop. A bell tinkled

on the door. A pretty sound prompted Lisa to turn and look at the door. A delicate set of chimes hung from a pewter replica of an orca. Each chime had a little charm hooked to the bottom; a tiny starfish, a seashell, a fish, and a seagull.

Thinking of her son, a catch tugged at her heart, and she remembered the sweatshirt tucked into the bottom of her suitcase. Certain they'd see whales at some point on this trip, she'd brought it to feel close to Cody.

"Excuse me, lady?"

Feeling a rough hand poking at her arm, Lisa looked up at an older gentleman. Only then did she realize she still stood in the doorway to the gift shop staring, albeit blankly, at the whale chimes.

"You gonna shop or what? You're making it awful hard for people to come in and out of the store."

Lisa looked around in embarrassment. The only one who seemed upset was this man. Still, people watched.

"I'm so sorry." She stepped aside. Ignoring the stares, she went to the counter and asked the clerk if they had any more chimes. While she waited, she picked up a novel from the rack near the counter and a bundle of brightly colored tulips from the refrigerated flower case.

On the way back to the room, she ducked into one of the many restaurants and ordered a take-out breakfast for Joe.

When Lisa arrived back at the room, her hands were full. She tried to juggle the tray of food, her purse, her book, her package with the wind chimes, and the bundle of tulips, all the while fishing her key card out of her pocket. She'd stuck it there earlier, to try and avoid this problem. Before she could stop them, the flowers slid to the floor.

"I'll get them for you, lady." She could tell without looking that the cheerful voice belonged to a little boy, and from the corner of her eye, Lisa saw a flash of sandy blond hair. *Cody!*

Of course it wasn't possible, but for just a moment she couldn't bring herself to look. When she did, a young boy stared up at her. With blond hair and blue eyes like Cody, this little boy was much younger than her son. He was about six years old, and his wide smile tugged at her heart. Obviously proud of himself, he held out the slightly battered tulips.

"Thank you." Lisa reached out to take them from him.

"You want me to hold 'em for you while you open the door?"

"That would be nice. Thank you."

"I'll hold those other things, too, if you want."

Lisa smiled at the boy and handed him the wind chimes and her book. Then she balanced the food tray with one arm while she inserted the key in the door. She held it open with her foot and took the flowers and other items from the little boy. He looked at her expectantly as if he hoped to come inside. "My husband's sleeping, so I have to be really quiet," she whispered. "But thank you for your help."

"You're welcome." The boy grinned up at her. "See ya!" With that, he scrambled down the hall.

As she let the door close quietly behind her, Lisa couldn't help but hope she'd see the little boy again.

Joe still slept restlessly. If only he would let her comfort him. She didn't want to push him, though. He wanted to be left alone. If helping him meant leaving him alone, she'd leave him alone. Surely, she could find a quiet spot on one of the decks somewhere and read her book. It didn't mean she had to like it, but for now it might be the best thing. She set the food and flowers on the table then went to the closet and tucked the wind chimes away. After grabbing her new book, she headed toward the door again. At the last minute, she turned back and plucked one deep purple parrot tulip from the vase then placed it on top of the lid covering Joe's food.

As she walked out the door, she couldn't help but wonder if it would hold the same meaning for Joe as it did for her.

****

A dozen good smells wafted in the air. Fragrant, tantalizing, all of them were Lisa. Shampoo, hair spray, deodorant, powder, each scent was a little different. All combined to create a wonderful scent belonging solely to her. They were the same fragrances that filled the air last night and made sure Lisa never left his thoughts.

She was here, and he had to accept it. That didn't mean he had to like it.

Of course, deep down on some level of his consciousness, he was happy she was here. OK, maybe that was stretching it. But some part of his soul recognized that her presence filled a small bit of the emptiness.

He'd had a lot of time to think last night while he tossed and turned. He remembered something Mike said that day he kept preaching about closure. The same day he suggested Joe should file for divorce. That Joe didn't really love Lisa. If he did, he'd help her find closure. Joe wasn't sure how a divorce equated to closure, but Mike said she'd be able to move on and find someone who could make her happy since Joe obviously couldn't.

Lisa had changed her mind about coming on the cruise. He couldn't really fault her for that. More than he did, Lisa deserved to be here finding closure. And could he, in all good conscience, interfere with her finding it? Plain and simple: no. It wouldn't be right.

Which meant he had to let her find what she was looking for, instead of fighting with her about being here. He couldn't act sullen and stubborn. Maybe he should even help make it enjoyable, so when she received the divorce papers she would at least have found closure over Cody's death. Maybe that would give him one less regret in his life.

But what would happen to his heart in the meantime?

Joe peeked one eye open, half expecting her to be sitting there staring at him. Much to his relief she wasn't. Having spent a restless night thinking of nothing but being in the same room with her, and how he would survive in her presence for the next two weeks, it was too much to hope she'd changed her mind and found other accommodations.

Of course she wouldn't. The determination he'd glimpsed in her eyes last night pretty much promised she wouldn't go away until she accomplished her goal. And Joe was certain of her goal. Him. He'd have to steel his nerves and dig in deep because as much as he'd love to just take her in his arms and make everything better, he couldn't.

That she still cared didn't surprise him. Lisa loved fiercely and never gave her heart conditionally. It would take a real slap in the face—the divorce papers—to get her to give up on him.

The thought of the pain it would cause her twisted his stomach in knots. He was so sorry. Sorry for everything. Who knew seventeen years ago that their marriage would end this way?

As teenagers, they'd been so full of hope for the future, so full of dreams. He never imagined he'd become such a slave to his career and put everyone dear to him on the back burner.

On his way to the shower, Joe noticed a covered tray on the table. Breakfast. Next to it sat a vase of brightly colored tulips. Courtesy of his wife, no doubt. He sure hadn't noticed them last night.

One tulip, the color of a ripe grape, lay across the lid.

A feeling of dread settled in his throat, and he continued toward the shower. If he hadn't been sure of her motive before, he certainly was now.

Grape parrot tulips had decorated the small country cabin on Campbell Lake where they'd spent their honeymoon. Lisa fell in love with the tulips. She ordered dozens of bulbs and planted them along the walkway of their first small house. She wasn't going to make this easy. Not one little bit.

She was trying to get him to feel things. Remember things. Determined not to let it work, Joe turned his back on the loving gesture and headed for the shower.

The blast of water felt good, but it wasn't strong enough to wash away his guilt over the hurt he'd see in Lisa's eyes when she discovered he'd ignored her breakfast tray.

When he finished in the shower, Joe tried not to notice the intimate way his toothbrush sat on the counter next to Lisa's. The way his deodorant was lined up next to hers. The little bottles and cans that made her smell so good were neatly set out on the counter.

He finished dressing, irritated for noticing so many small things. Even more irritating, though, was the guilt.

Joe couldn't stand the pain encompassing Lisa. It was one of the reasons he'd stopped going home after work. Being obligated to work was one thing—it helped him shove aside the emotional pain of Cody's loss. But once the workday was over and it was time to go home to Lisa, the dread would start building inside his gut. She was sad. And he...he was guilty. That's why it was so impossible for him to live up to his obligations as a husband and help his wife through the tragedy. It was becoming more and more difficult to keep from shedding tears himself.

He couldn't bear to wipe one more tear from her eyes, couldn't bear to wrap her in his arms and offer his shoulder any longer.

So...if eating the food she brought would keep the hurt from her eyes, he'd eat it.

Sitting alone at the table, Joe pulled the cover off the tray of food. As the smells of French toast and bacon teased his senses, he looked around the little room, thinking about what today—this trip—would have been like if he hadn't made a stupid, selfish decision that altered their lives forever. Cody would have been here, laughing, eager. Lisa's eyes wouldn't look so haunted, and her face wouldn't be so thin.

Oh, Lisa, I'm so sorry.

It shouldn't have been that way.

If only he'd been what a husband and father

should be. He'd been lousy at both. His wife would be so much better off without him in her life. She deserved her chance at happiness and the way to find it sure wasn't with him.

****

Exhausted after exploring the shops and salons on all the different decks, Lisa finally plopped herself down on a cushy lounge chair and stared out at the water. She didn't know what deck she was on, but she was tired and didn't really care.

This would be tougher than she'd originally thought. Joe was her heart, her soul, her life. She had to make him realize that before it was too late. Judging by his reaction to her presence, "too late" wasn't that far off, and it terrified her. Would he spend the entire cruise like this?

"Things are never as bad as they seem, dear."

Startled out of her self-pitying thoughts, Lisa looked up to see a pleasant-faced older woman standing next to her.

"May I?" The woman pointed to the chair next to Lisa.

Lisa nodded, unsure about wanting to converse with someone right now. "Please, be my guest." She waved at the empty chair even though she didn't mean it.

"Ah." The woman sighed as she sat down. "These chairs really are comfortable."

"Yes, they are."

Lisa looked out at the water. Perhaps if she didn't engage the woman in conversation, she would simply go away. She seemed nice enough, but Lisa had too much on her mind to get to know someone right now. Though she now had her blossoming friendship with Rose, she'd never really been good at close relationships. Not with anyone but Joe.

"Jessica Lane." The woman extended her hand, and Lisa had no choice but to take it. She didn't want to seem rude. The woman's firm, warm clasp took Lisa by surprise, and she could almost feel the caring emanating from the older woman.

That was, of course, ridiculous. Kind and friendly though she might be, the woman was a complete stranger.

"Lisa Kendall." She waited for what seemed to be the proper amount of time and withdrew her hand.

"Is this your first cruise?" Jessica's green eyes seemed to sparkle behind her thick glasses.

"Yes. And you?"

Jessica nodded and leaned forward in a confiding manner. "To tell you the truth, it's my first trip anywhere."

Lisa looked at her, in awe. "Really?"

"Really. My husband and I were always too busy working to take a trip. Not that I regret anything," she added quickly.

It was amazing that a woman her age was taking her first trip, and all alone. But Lisa wasn't up for small talk, especially with a stranger, so she simply nodded and looked away.

"I saw you in the gift store earlier."

This ship was so big. How odd the woman would not only notice her in the gift store but then run into her on one of the observation decks.

"You were buying tulips."

Lisa nodded. "I bought them for my husband."

Had Joe found the tulips yet? She hoped they would bring a smile to his face and remind him of a time when they'd been happy. Would he understand their meaning? To her they symbolized their wedding vows, the home they made, and the life they shared. She wasn't giving all of it up just yet.

"That's why I recognized you when I saw you sitting here."

Embarrassed, Lisa realized she didn't hear everything Jessica had said to her. "I'm sorry, what?"

"The tulips. My husband and I owned a bulb farm in Skagit Valley. Other people traveled to us to see the tulips we grew every spring."

"You owned a bulb farm?"

"I still do, actually. But it's becoming more and more difficult to run all by myself."

"My husband and I used to drive over to Skagit Valley every spring to see the tulip fields when they bloomed. Joe used to take his camera and take pictures." Lisa sighed, thankful for something pleasant to think about. She closed her eyes, envisioning field after field of colorful tulips. Every spring they stretched across the landscape for miles, ribbons of color, like one of God's rainbows across the sky. "I can see how that would be a difficult business to run by yourself."

"Frank and I were quite content working our farm, hiring school kids to help us out since we didn't have any of our own." Jessica gazed out at the water, a wistful look on her face.

Thinking of Cody, Lisa heart constricted. What would it have been like not to have had him in her life?

"Now Frank's gone, and I have to pull myself out of my comfort zone and see some of the world.

Otherwise, I'll just pine away. Funny thing, though. Frank's been gone a few years, and it wasn't until recently that I had this sudden urge to travel. First thing I decided to do was come on this cruise. A cruise is something I'd never even thought about in my entire life."

Lisa didn't know what to say. What it would be like to be Jessica's age—maybe early seventies—and on a trip, alone? It was likely to happen, too, given the lack of response from Joe.

"You said you and your husband used to drive to see the tulip fields. So you must live in Washington, too. Where are you from?"

"Whidbey Island."

"Oh. Not far away at all. We're practically neighbors." Jessica's wide smile indicated she hoped she'd found a new friend.

Lisa couldn't help but smile back.

"You said you bought the tulips for your husband." Jessica glanced around. "I'd love to meet him."

Lisa cringed a little inside before she answered. "My husband is back in the room. He doesn't—"

"Cabin."

"Sorry?" Lisa blinked. Though surprised, she was glad for the unexpected interruption. It saved her from talking about Joe.

"You called it a room." Jessica stared at Lisa, unblinking though a hint of a smile played at the corners of her mouth. "We're on a ship, dear. I believe the correct term is *cabin*."

Despite her dim outlook, Lisa couldn't help but laugh. "I stand corrected."

"Sorry." Jessica's lashes fluttered behind her

glasses, much like a naughty child who didn't really mean it. "Bad little habit. Interrupting and correcting. I'm a little compulsive."

"It's perfectly fine." Lisa meant it. Her own mother had been that way.

"Miss Jessica!" The little boy who'd helped Lisa with the tulips earlier skidded to a stop in front of them. He looked from Jessica to Lisa and smiled. "Hi, again."

"Do you two know each other?" Jessica arched her eyebrows, the question clear on her face.

"Yup." The boy graced Jessica with a grin that almost stretched to both of his ears. "I helped her with her flowers when they crashed to the ground."

Lisa looked to Jessica. "I was carrying too much." She turned to the little boy and smiled. "I'm Lisa. What's your name?"

"This is Brandon." Jessica smiled at the boy before he could answer. "He and his father are staying just a few doors down from me."

"Right near the room where I helped you." Brandon's blue eyes twinkled as he grinned even wider. A breeze picked up just then and rustled through his hair. Lisa ached to reach out and brush it down with her hand. The back of her eyes burned, and her heart lurched.

"I guess we're all neighbors then." Trying to hide her emotions, she spoke a little too loud, and Jessica glanced at her.

"Are you all right?"

"I'm fine, just happy to officially meet Brandon."

"Ohh-kaay. If you say so." Jessica made it obvious she didn't believe her. "Where's your dad, Brandon?"

"He's back at our cabin. He told me he needed

some quiet time. I'm supposed to stay on this deck, and if I want to go somewhere else, I need to tell him."

"Well, now Brandon, you're a good boy for giving your dad some time alone. You be careful." Jessica leaned forward and touched his arm. "And mind your dad. If you've been gone for a while, you might want to let him know you're doing as he says."

"Sure thing, Miss Jessica." Brandon waved as he ran off.

"He and his father ate dinner with me last night," Jessica said once Brandon was out of sight. "Are you and your husband planning to eat in the dining room tonight?"

Lisa thought of the blue dress she'd wanted to wear for Joe. She had little to no chance of getting him into that dining room.

She shook her head. "I seriously doubt Joe will want to get dressed up for a formal dinner. In fact, I don't think he even brought a suit with him."

"You mean, you don't know?" Jessica tipped her head and peered over the top of her glasses.

Lisa glanced away from Jessica then back again. "I-I wasn't there when Joe packed."

Jessica nodded as though she understood perfectly, but her eyes were sharp and gave away her suspicion that all was not right with Lisa's marriage.

Uncomfortable, Lisa went back to staring out at the water and caught her breath. It was as if the ship was slowly moving through a narrow maze of rugged snow-peaked mountains and evergreen-covered islands. The beauty of it awed her, and she wished she could get Joe to share it with her.

This must be the Inside Passage. Shamefully, she didn't really know for sure. She hadn't spent much time reading up on the actual cruise. Her priorities had been all about getting Joe to go and then finding the nerve to follow him. Too bad they couldn't enjoy this view together.

"There's more than one dining room on this ship, and the one where I'm having dinner isn't as formal as you might think. Even though it's not *the* formal dining room, it's still very nice. But you and your husband don't have to dress to the nines to eat there."

Lisa tore her gaze from a pair of kayakers setting for shore on one of the islands. She sighed and shifted uncomfortably before she turned back to Jessica.

"Oh, I don't think Joe will be comfortable eating in the dining room, whether it's formal or not." She tried to keep her tone light but knew the older woman saw right through her when she reached out and squeezed Lisa's hand.

"I apologize again. Nosy to a fault. That's what my Frank always used to say. He told me it would get me into trouble someday, and he was right. Here I am making you uncomfortable." She looked sincerely distressed. Had her Frank been overly critical of her?

The thought that someone could hurt this sweet elderly woman made Lisa angry.

"It's OK, really," Lisa was quick to assure her. "I didn't take it that way at all. My husband isn't up to sightseeing. In fact, he doesn't even want me here."

Jessica leaned forward with interest, and Lisa shrank back in her chair horrified at herself. Why had she revealed so much? Just to make someone else feel better? She *so* did not want to talk about it.

"I'm sorry, dear." Jessica gently touched her arm. OK, maybe it was compassion that flickered in Jessica's eyes, not interest. Either way, it made Lisa uncomfortable. She wasn't used to being so intimate with other people. Rose was the only one she confided in.

"Do you two have kids?"

Again Lisa's heart constricted. "One. A boy. Cody."

"That's good, dear. At least you have someone to hold you together. Kids are the perfect way to bring parents together again. Things will work out; you'll see."

"He's dead." Even Lisa winced at her blunt tone. "He was killed in a car accident several months ago."

Lisa had been born late in her parents' lives. Had they still been alive, they would be about the same age as Jessica. She missed her mother so much. Her parents would have helped her and Joe through this ordeal. Lisa couldn't even turn to Joe's mother, because she had disowned him when he married Lisa. Perhaps that was why she was so drawn to Jessica, why she blurted out something so personal to a total stranger.

"Oh, my dear, I am so very sorry." Jessica squeezed Lisa's hand. Compassion filled her eyes and her gentle grandmotherly apple cheeks punctuated a smile of understanding.

Tears brimmed in Lisa's eyes and Jessica offered her a hanky from her jacket pocket.

"No, thank you." Lisa shook her head. "I'll be fine."

"It's all right to let it out, you know." Jessica reached over and gently patted her hand.

It had never been all right around Joe. Tears scared the daylights out of him. Emotions petrified him. Especially *her* emotions. He'd proven that by not coming around after that weekend he'd taken her away for her birthday. They'd frightened him away from coming home at night and into sleeping at the office. Lisa knew all about the damage that came from letting tears and emotions flow.

"I—I've got to go." Lisa couldn't get out of the chair fast enough and nearly tripped. Jessica reached out a hand to help steady her, a shocked look on her face. "I'm so sorry." Horrified that she'd hurt this kind and lonely woman's feelings, Lisa covered Jessica's hand with her own. "It really was nice meeting you."

Jessica nodded. "Perhaps we'll meet again. Maybe tonight, in the dining room?"

"Yes, perhaps. But, to tell you the truth, Jessica, as much as I'd love to eat dinner with you, if Joe won't go to the dining room, I won't either. My first priority is him, not me. And I doubt he'll want to eat there."

"I understand dear. But have a little faith. I'll ask the steward to make sure you're seated at my table if you are able to make it."

"Thank you, Jessica. I hope to see you then, but I doubt it. Maybe we'll meet around here again. If not, enjoy the rest of your trip. It was lovely meeting you."

"You, too, dear. I'll be praying for you."

Before she headed back to her room…cabin, Lisa smiled fondly at the older woman. As Lisa walked away, she heard Jessica whisper, "It really will be all right."

A shiver snaked down her spine, and she hoped with all her heart that Jessica was right. But she had a sick sort of feeling things would never be all right again.

6

The door opened, and Joe looked up.

Lisa stepped into the cabin. "Not hungry, huh?"

Joe picked up the fork and pushed at a syrup-soaked cold piece of French toast, took a sip of lukewarm coffee, and shook his head. "Sorry." He was unable to look her in the eyes.

"Don't be. I know what it's like to lack the heart to eat. But Joe—" She placed her hand over his. Her warm and tender touch seeped through him to tickle the edges of his heart. He closed his eyes and breathed in deep, not knowing how he would get through the next forty or so years without it.

"Joe, you can't starve yourself. It won't bring him back."

Joe gave her a long look, assessing the thinness of her face and arms. He thought back to her comment about starving.

"What about you? Have you been eating? You sure don't look like it."

"This isn't about me. It's about you."

"So it's all right for you to be concerned about me but not vice versa?" he asked.

"Lip service, Joe. If you were interested in me, you would have shown it long before now. You're only trying to divert the attention from yourself."

Had he imagined it, or was there a little spark in her eyes?

"Do you want to go for a walk on deck? I saw some of the scenery, and it's absolutely beautiful." A nervous smile played on her pink lips.

Uh-oh. Had she taken their tiny conversation and turned it into something more? *Careful.* He couldn't do anything to make her think things were going back to the way they were or even that he would go home with her at the end of the cruise.

He pulled his hand from hers so fast he heard her ring slap against the table.

"Sorry." Though he spoke quickly, he meant it. "Are you OK?" Here he went hurting her again.

"I'm fine."

But he knew she wasn't.

Avoiding her gaze, he put the silver lid back on the tray. "Are we supposed to put this outside?" At Lisa's nod, he started toward the door.

Stepping in front of him, Lisa reached for the tray. "Here, I'll take it."

But she made no move to leave the room. She stood there watching while Joe pulled his laptop out of the leather carrying case and set it on the table.

Joe booted up the computer, waited for a connection, and settled back in the chair. He could feel her blue eyes watching his every move. The silence in the room was so heavy he could practically hear her thoughts of condemnation. If she had any idea about the e-mail he was about to send to Mike, confirming his plans for divorce and giving his okay to file the papers he'd signed before he'd left the office, she'd want to heap hot coals over his head.

Finally, putting the tray back on the table, right next to his laptop, she asked the question he expected. "Are you going to shut yourself off the entire trip?"

He shrugged and focused on the computer screen. For some reason, it seemed to infuriate her.

"Do you think it's been easy sitting at home with all those memories day and night *by myself*? Maybe you forgot everything when you walked away, but I sure didn't. Cody was my son, too. I hurt as much as you do. And just like you need to find some sense of peace in all of this, Joe, so do I. Maybe I didn't isolate myself and abandon the people I supposedly love, but maybe, just maybe, I need to be here as much as you do."

For Joe, it was a painful truth. He was responsible for the sadness that oozed from her heart. Even before Cody died, all he did was work. He knew exactly what it cost him. If he hadn't made his job his god, none of this would have happened.

"We're supposed to find the joy in our sorrows, the blessings in the storm, praise God in all circumstances. You're not doing that. You've taken your eyes off the Lord. You've shut yourself off from everyone who loves you. You've turned into a lonely, bitter man." She stopped and gasped as if unable to believe what she'd just said.

"Joe, I'm so sorry." She reached for him, but he shrugged away. Lisa nodded slowly. "Fine." She pulled her hand back. "Have things your way."

"What do you want me to say? That I'm sorry I *abandoned* you?" He deliberately emphasized the word and watched as she rubbed at her arm where it had been broken in the accident. Though long since healed, she tended to rub the broken spot when she was upset. Unfortunately, upsetting her couldn't be helped. Not this time. "Do you want me to tell you I'm glad you're here?"

"Only if you mean it." Lisa stopped rubbing her arm, picked the tray back up, and went out the door.

Joe waited until the door slammed shut before he whispered, "I do."

He didn't want to think about what those two little words meant, and he certainly didn't want to ponder the fact that the sight of his ring on her finger and the touch of her hand on his made his heart beat just a little differently.

****

Outside their room, Lisa set the food tray on the floor in the hall. Then she leaned against the cool wood of the door separating her from Joe.

A sick sort of feeling engulfed her. She didn't want to think about the reason. Her heart pounded and her chest constricted. She took a slow deep breath to keep the uncomfortable feeling at bay.

It was a deep well of emptiness, as if God were far away from her. This wasn't the first time she'd experienced it. And because of that, what right did she have to use those words against Joe the way she had? He might have taken his eyes off God, but she couldn't feel Him. She could no longer sense the peace He'd once filled her with. "Please, Lord, help me find it again. I need to know You're here with me."

Utterly ashamed and sick about what she'd said to Joe, Lisa didn't know whether to pace the deck or fall down on her knees and cry. She refused to give in to the emotion. She had to stay strong and focused, keep her eye on the goal: pull Joe out of this. Then, and only then, could she save her marriage.

Oh, Joe. How could she have used guilt on him like

that? Guilt. On a man who was already torturing himself with it.

"Forgive me, Lord," she prayed. "Take away the sting of my words."

The very last thing she wanted to do was hurt Joe or instill more guilt in him. He'd heaped a big enough load of it on himself.

She'd meant for this to be a sanctuary for him, and here she'd added to his grief.

Everything was such a mess.

Helping Joe was her priority. Helping him *and* getting him back. Even though it seemed impossible, she couldn't—*wouldn't*—give up on him.

She truly did feel like she needed this as much as he did. And her reasons weren't just because she'd hoped to get Joe to come home, but also so they could feel closer to Cody. If they took this trip their son had looked forward to, wouldn't it help them say good-bye?

She pictured Joe inside the room, becoming more and more absorbed in whatever was on the computer screen.

For a minute, back in the room, Lisa thought Joe was coming around. When she'd returned to find him sitting there with a fork in his hand, eating breakfast, she'd had a moment of hope. But her hope was short lived, shriveled like a grape in the California sun when she'd sat across from the table and he'd shut her out of his pain.

Was it too much to hope he'd accept her presence and actually want to enjoy two weeks with her? She didn't think it was, though she knew she had a better chance of convincing Rose to step foot into a church.

Lisa wished she could run back inside the room

and slam the laptop shut. She wanted to shake him back to reality, kiss the sadness from his eyes, and get him to come back home with her. But he'd most likely have no part of it. All she could do was pray and ask the Lord to help Joe see that they needed to grieve for their son together. He needed to come home. "Please let him see that, Lord. Please."

"Let's do this together," Lisa silently willed from her heart to Joe's. If only she could make him understand.

****

With Lisa gone, Joe paced the small room. She spoke the truth when she said he'd abandoned her and isolated himself. He'd shut everyone out so he could pretend he didn't have issues to deal with.

But were they easier to deal with alone?

Part of him wanted to rush to the door and call her back. But he didn't. He couldn't. No matter how much he wanted to hold Lisa and make her his wife again, he couldn't. He didn't deserve her, and she certainly didn't deserve to be saddled with him.

If only he could turn back time, go back to the place where Cody was a newborn. "Why, God? Why won't You turn back time? Why won't You let me start over? I'll do my best. I promise I'll be the best father and best husband ever. I just don't want to see that pain in Lisa's eyes anymore."

It couldn't happen. In fact, why was he even talking to God? As if *He* even listened. If God listened to him, the accident never would have happened in the first place.

No. That wasn't fair. It wasn't God's fault. It was

his fault. *Joe's.* He was the one who messed up. He had the chance and didn't take it. He's the one who made work more important than his family.

God wouldn't help him now. He wasn't worth it. He deserved everything he got.

But Cody didn't. Neither did Lisa.

****

When Lisa finally found the courage and strength to face Joe, she slowly opened the door.

"Joe?"

Just the way she'd left him, he sat in the chair with his laptop. She could tell by his expression, he wasn't seeing whatever was on the screen. She could also tell that he heard her but had no intention of answering.

"Joe, I'm sorry. I—the things I said—please don't hate me. I don't even know why I said what I did."

"Because you meant it." The cynicism in his voice saddened her.

"No. I didn't express myself very well. You need to grieve in whatever way you feel. And there's no set timetable. I used a poor choice of words. I'm so sorry."

"It doesn't matter, Lisa."

"Yes, it does. Look at me."

When he still didn't look up, she went over to the closet and pulled out her bags. She unzipped one with fury and began pulling at her clothing on the hangers.

"What are you doing?"

Lisa turned around to find Joe watching her from across the room. He'd closed the laptop and stood next to the table. His brown eyes gazed at her intently.

"I—I made a mistake," she said, flustered by the way he stared at her. "You were right. You do need to be alone. I'm going to see if they have another room available."

"They don't." His tone spoke volumes. "I checked."

Another piece of her heart broke.

"There has to be someplace I can sleep until we get to Ketchikan. Then I'll see about getting a plane home."

"But you're afraid to fly."

"I'm more afraid of saying something else to hurt you than I am of getting on an airplane. You don't deserve it."

In two strides, Joe was across the room. With gentleness Lisa hadn't seen from him in a long time, he took the bags from her and put them back in the closet. He even went so far as to re-hang the one outfit she'd managed to tear from its hanger.

"What are you doing?"

"Lisa, I'm sorry."

Her breath caught in her throat, and she eyed him warily.

"It was rude of me to try to make you leave. You're right. You do need to say good-bye the same way I do. I have no right to tell you otherwise."

Did this mean he was ready to find closure at the loss of their son? Had the Lord answered her prayer already? Hope blossomed within her.

"Joe?"

"Let's start over."

Her heart pounded.

"How is Rose?"

Lisa blinked at the change in conversation.

"After you mentioned her last night, I wondered how she was doing."

"She's not good. She tries, but she's not..." Lisa

pressed her lips together and shook her head. How did she explain one person's inability to cope with grief to another person who was having the same difficulty?

"I'm glad she has you for a friend." Joe's tone was quiet. "I'm sure you're good for her."

"I don't know." Lisa shook her head. "I feel so helpless. Like there's something more I should be doing for her."

"You can't fix everyone, Lisa."

Was that what she tried to do? Fix everyone? "I know that. I just want to help. But it's really hard to help Rose because she doesn't go to church."

"Neither do I." Joe's broken whisper infused Lisa with guilt.

Why had she brought up church? Joe stopped going months ago, and though she tried several times to get him to back to church, he adamantly refused.

"I know. I'm sorry." She didn't want to say anything to undo this fragile truce they had. "I didn't mean—"

"I know you didn't. It's all right. Don't force it." He sounded so calm, Lisa could scarcely believe it. They were actually having a conversation about church, and Joe wasn't defensive. She almost collapsed with relief. Here she'd been so afraid he'd turned his back on God.

Did he still believe? She wanted to ask but didn't. "Rose doesn't believe in God."

"Don't give up on her." He spoke quietly, and Lisa couldn't help but hope he was also asking her not to give up on him.

"I won't," she assured him. Nor would she ever give up on him. Ever.

"I'm sorry about the way I've acted. I know I

overreacted to your being here." He met her gaze. "I was embarrassed at the way you found me yesterday. You know…the things I said when I first woke up and didn't know you were here. I was surprised to find you here. Maybe even a little…" he swallowed hard and shook his head.

"Joe," she whispered around the painful lump in her throat. "Were you glad to see me?"

Before he answered, he turned away from her. "I can't answer that honestly, but believe it or not, there was some part of me that wished I didn't have to do this by myself."

Who did you want to do this with? She wanted to ask the question, but she was too afraid of what his response would be.

Lisa took a deep breath as Joe stepped closer. Everything would be OK after all. She let out the breath, embarrassed that it sounded so much like a sigh, and prepared to take Joe into her arms. Instead, he brushed past her toward the bathroom.

"I know you need to grieve." He spoke from the bathroom doorway, his tone of voice a lot sharper than it had been a minute ago. "The same way you keep telling me I need to grieve. You're here. There's nothing I can do about it. But don't tell me how to spend my time. There's nothing you can do to make me enjoy myself. I suggest you leave me alone."

"Joe, I—" She started toward him, but he held up his hand.

"Look, do what you want. Just don't involve me in it. Are we clear?"

He sounded so dejected and distressed Lisa wanted to throw her arms around him and soothe his hurts away. Of course she didn't, couldn't. She'd be met with resentment, and she didn't want Joe to resent her. She only wanted him to love her.

"Perfectly," she whispered as the door shut behind him.

Feeling like a fool, Lisa tried to rein in her emotions. For one silly moment, she thought things would be OK. Was it so wrong to want that? Was it wrong to hope?

****

While Joe was in the shower, Lisa sat on the floor of the closet and unzipped one of her bags. It was the only bag she hadn't unpacked. It held personal things, things she didn't want Joe to see yet. Bits and pieces of their life together. Things she'd hoped to share with him once he agreed to come home and be her husband again.

But things weren't going as she planned, and she prayed it wasn't a sign of things to come.

Please, God, let this work out for us.

What if it never happened? She needed to face facts. Joe didn't want her here. He had even checked to see if another room might be available for her. Pain squeezed her throat making it difficult to swallow. She struggled to keep the tears at bay. She didn't want Joe to come out of the shower and find her crying.

Maybe she shouldn't be so quick to give up. Didn't he all but say he was glad she was here? Well, maybe she shouldn't go that far, but it certainly seemed like that's what he'd been about to say before he turned around and told her to leave him alone.

Lisa shook her head. She wanted to hope, but confusion warred in her heart. Then a stray thought hit her. It was possible Joe was confused as well.

As she rummaged through the suitcase, Lisa's mind whirled. Maybe, just maybe, she could find a way to help him deal with his confusion. Maybe together they could find a way to help each other.

Slowly, she pulled out her whale shirt. Cody's too. For just a minute, she imagined he was here instead of heaven. Did God let the spirit of our loved ones visit once in a while? Is that why she sensed Cody's presence sometimes? If He did then it was an almost certainty Cody was here with her now. Or perhaps it was merely wishful thinking and a heavy dose of her imagination.

She placed the shirts side-by-side. Lovingly, she ran her hand across the picture Cody had drawn. Tears threatened again, this time burning the back of her eyes. She wouldn't be able to hold them back much longer. It hurt to swallow, and her entire chest ached with emotion. She picked up his shirt and pressed her face against it, reveling in the little boy scent it still held. For a minute, it really did seem like he was here with her.

"Oh, Cody, come back to me," she whispered.

7

When Joe came back into the room, Lisa sat on the floor in front of the closet. The doors were open, two shirts spread on the floor. He recognized the artwork that graced them. One of Cody's drawings. Lisa had somehow transferred them onto the sweatshirts. Why had she brought them here?

"Lisa?"

It took a heartbeat too long before she looked up, and in that space of time, Joe knew she'd been crying and struggled to hide it from him.

When she did turn and look up at him, she situated her body in such a way as if to shield him from seeing the shirts.

She thinks she's protecting me.

Again, guilt stabbed him and made him feel unworthy; affirming once more that he'd made the right decision.

"What are you doing?"

"Just...repacking."

"Lisa, you don't have to hide it from me."

"I'm not."

"What's that?" He pointed to the small paper-wrapped package on the floor.

"Just a little something I bought at the gift store."

Before he could see what it was, she'd wrapped it in Cody's shirt and stuffed it in her suitcase. Just as quickly, she folded her matching shirt and put it on top of Cody's. Then she zipped the suitcase and jumped up.

With a jerk, she grabbed a sweater from a hanger and smiled brightly—too brightly in his opinion.

****

Lisa tried to avoid looking into Joe's eyes, and struggled to keep her emotions from giving her away.

"Lisa, are you all right?" He sounded sincere, if a bit tentative.

"I'm fine." He had enough to deal with, without adding her pain to the mix. "I'm going for a walk."

"Oh."

With one hand on the doorknob and the other clutching a light blue sweater, Lisa finally looked at Joe. The concern etching the corners of his eyes was real and touched her heart. She started to ask him to join her then stopped herself.

"I promised to leave you alone," she said softly. "I keep my promises." This didn't mean she was giving up on him, though.

His brow rose, and his mouth opened as if to say something.

She paused for just a moment, hoping he'd ask to join her. When he didn't say anything she let herself into the hall and quietly shut the door behind her, praying she'd been able to conceal her disappointment.

In the corridor, she leaned against the wall and closed her eyes. The hope that he'd come after her refused to die even five minutes later when she trudged toward the elevator. She stared at the door to their room longingly as she waited for the elevator to open. Standing inside, she watched for him, hoping he'd come out just as the doors closed.

Trying not to feel sad, she pressed the button for the Stargazer Deck. As a show of good faith, she would keep her word and let him be.

For now.

Eventually, she hoped, he would come around. If he didn't, Lisa wasn't sure what she'd do, but she wasn't about to give up. She had faith. God knew her needs. He would make a way. She had to believe it.

No. She *did* believe it.

****

Lisa went back to the deck where she'd met Jessica. Of all the places she'd been on the ship, it was the most inviting, the most comfortable—a place of belonging. And the view from there was gorgeous.

White mist danced through the treetops of the green islands and seemed to create a welcome pathway for the ship as they slowly made their way toward Alaska. Canoes, kayaks, and small boats were scattered here and there. She'd never seen so many hawks, eagles, and herons at one time.

"You have such a beautiful creation, Lord," she whispered the prayer. "Help me not take it for granted when I'm so caught up in this misery with Joe. I want to feel Your presence. I need to know You're here with me in this peaceful place. I'm begging You, please give me just a small bit of that peace. And please, Lord, please help Joe find it, too."

People milled around, and Lisa tried not to notice the one difference between them and her—she was alone. And trying very hard not to feel hopeless.

Would she ever get through to Joe? Or would their

marriage forever be stuck in this dreary limbo? Though neither of them believed in divorce, Joe was no longer the man she married. Perhaps his beliefs had changed. Maybe he was waiting for her to make the first move — which, of course, she'd never do.

Divorce was not an option. At least, not where she was concerned.

As she wandered around the Skygazer Deck, Lisa's troubled thoughts drained the energy right out of her. Just as she went to find the lounge chairs she'd sat in earlier that day with Jessica, Lisa overheard one word that stopped her in her tracks and sent her heart racing.

Whales. Word was buzzing that a pod was up ahead, and the ship would be coming up on them in about twenty minutes. It gave her enough time to get back to the cabin and tell Joe.

Would he want to see them? Of course he would. Cody had drawn so many pictures of them for his dad. Still, Lisa had mixed feelings about going back to the cabin to tell him about the sighting. She'd be breaking her word to leave him alone. But, surely, he'd want to see them.

Together they could see what their son so badly wanted to see, and it would be almost as if he were here with them.

As she hurried to tell Joe before the whales were gone, she found her energy returning.

When she stepped off the elevator on Denali Deck, Brandon came around the corner so fast he couldn't stop. Lisa couldn't get out of the way in time. He slammed into her with all the force of a Little Leaguer sliding into home with the game on the line.

Though the impact hurt, it didn't compare to the

pain wedged in her heart when she looked into his face.

She gasped. She knew that look, the enthusiasm. She'd seen it on Cody's face so many times.

Cody. Oh, Cody. She missed him so much. Why couldn't he be here with her? Surprised by the sudden pain, she tried furiously to blink back the looming tears.

"Sorry, Miss Lisa," Brandon mumbled.

"Hey, it's OK," Lisa assured him. She reached out and touched his shoulder and found herself strangely comforted by the feel of his flannel shirt under her fingers. "Are you all right?"

He nodded vigorously. "I've gotta find my dad."

"What's your hurry?" A bittersweet smile tugged at the corners of Lisa's mouth as she watched the eagerness light his face.

"I gotta tell him about the whales."

"Did you get to see them?"

"No." Brandon shook his head. "No one's seen 'em yet. But I'm gonna. I heard this lady say the captain thinks there's some real close. I gotta get my dad. Quick."

He was gone before Lisa could say another word.

Lisa's heart squeezed painfully. Brandon, adorable and exuberant, reminded her of what she'd lost. And he was about to witness what Cody never would, what he'd always wanted to see. Through tear-blurred eyes, she raced back to the cabin and burst through the door.

"Joe!" Heart thumping, she struggled to catch her breath. Too late, she realized she'd scared him.

He jumped up from his chair so fast the book he'd been reading dropped to the floor with a loud smack.

"What's wrong?"

"Whales," she gasped, nodding at the same time so he wouldn't worry. "We have to hurry."

"That's it? I thought something was wrong."

His reaction puzzled her. "What do you mean, 'that's it'? Seeing them in their natural habitat was Cody's dream."

"So?" He reached down to grab at the book, but his fingers just caught the edges, and the book toppled end-over-end. Just like their lives.

"Come on, Joe." In spite of the sense of urgency overwhelming her, Lisa softened her voice. "I want you to see them with me. For Cody."

"Cody's not here." The bitterness in his tone pierced her heart.

"I know he's not, but you are. You can't stop living. *Or feeling*." If the way he studied the book was any indication, that's exactly what he intended.

"You don't know anything about it."

Of course she did, and she could tell by the way he wouldn't meet her eyes, he *knew* she did.

"I know it hurts. But it's time to find a way to deal with the hurt."

As soon as she spoke the words, she wished she could take them back. She hadn't meant to sound so callous. Who was she to tell him when to deal with his grief?

Maybe if she hadn't shown up unannounced, he *would* be dealing with it. Once again doubts plagued her. She wanted to help him, not make things worse. "I'm sorry. I just thought it would help us feel closer to him. If Cody were still alive and he—"

"He's not." Joe's words were cold, flat.

"I know that." She clenched her fists. Desperation seized her. How could she get through to him? "Just listen for a minute. If Cody were still alive, and he couldn't be here, what would you do? What would he *want* you to do? I think he'd want you to see the whales and remember every detail and then tell him all about it. That's exactly what I intend to do."

"Watch the whales and then tell Cody?"

She swallowed hard. She hadn't meant to say that. "Yes."

"You talk to Cody?" He had a curious, questioning tone to his voice.

"Sometimes." Heat stole across her face. "Sometimes it's like he's still here, and I talk to him before I've even realized it."

He creased his brow and stared at her with a frown. Did he think she was crazy? She wasn't.

Lisa closed her mouth, not wanting him to worry about her any more than he already did. Even though Joe wanted to act as if he didn't care, he had to worry about her.

She approached him and hesitated, unsure of whether she was trying the right tact. "If I promise to stay here in the cabin, will you go up and see the whales?"

"No!" He reached down again and scooped up the book. Then he slammed it against his thigh. Lisa jumped, fighting back sudden tears.

A flicker of regret appeared to cross Joe's face. But it disappeared almost instantly. If it was regret, Joe managed to hide it before she could be sure. Then he said, "Do whatever you want. Just leave me alone."

Unable to respond, Lisa pressed her hands to her cheeks. Relieved to find no tears had spilled over, she let herself out the door without a backward glance.

****

Once again, Lisa found herself standing outside their cabin—alone. A sense of despair overwhelmed her. This day would only get worse.

The frightening blowup Joe displayed when she'd told him about the whales certainly wasn't what she'd expected, but logic told her his rage wasn't directed at her. Joe would never hurt her. Still, some deep-seated instinct hurried her out of there.

Still upset by the confrontation with Joe, she went right past the elevator until she found the stairwell where she took the stairs two at a time until she reached the Skygazer Deck.

Why she chose this deck, she couldn't say. Perhaps because it was fast becoming familiar to her while the rest of the ship seemed to be a huge intimidating void she wanted no part of. At least in this small corner of the ship, with its green plants and comforting furniture, she could see the view and feel almost at home.

Heading down the length of the deck, Lisa noted how empty it was. That was odd. There had been such a buzz about the whales before she'd gone to get Joe, she was certain everyone on the ship would be watching for them.

The occasional couple or family milled about, but they weren't even looking over the side as if there was something to see.

Had she missed them? Her hopes fell.

No. She refused to contemplate it. She *had* to see the whales. Not just for Cody but for herself.

Desperate now, heart hammering, Lisa looked for a way to cut across to the other side of the deck.

She ducked into a nearby lounge, cringing at the thick cloud of smoke and loud noise. Clearly she'd found one of the smoking areas. But there across the crowded place, a door opened to the opposite side of the ship.

Lisa dashed across the room and out the door.

Here she found the crowds. She wanted to raise her fist and punch the air in victory. Especially when she heard the loud chorus of ooohs and aaahs. But she wasn't outwardly demonstrative in front of other people. Call it shyness—she wasn't sure what else to call it. Either way, she kept her impulses to herself.

"Thank you, Lord," she prayed sincerely as she ran toward the crowd.

****

If Cody was still alive and he couldn't be here, what would you do? Lisa's words taunted Joe until he wanted to lash out and slam his fists into the wall. Frustrated, he paced around the cabin, sickened by the confrontation and the way he'd spoken to her. The hurt in those beautiful blue eyes was something he wouldn't soon forget. If ever.

Did she really talk to their son? She seemed nervous when she said it, as if she feared he'd think her crazy. He was glad she could find enough peace to believe that Cody heard her when she spoke to him. Glad and something else he had a hard time admitting even to himself. *Jealous.*

He longed to reach the place Lisa had, but she seemed to have found peace in knowing their son was in God's hands and that she'd see him again someday. Joe always thought it was something he believed, but when faced with the reality of death, his belief disintegrated. He'd give anything to have it back so he could close his eyes and picture his son in heaven.

Squeezing his eyes shut, Joe tried to imagine Cody happy in heaven, playing ball, swimming with the whales…seated at the feet of Jesus.

Nothing happened.

Panicked he tried again, needing to conjure his son's smiling face, to hear Cody's voice asking Joe to come throw the ball with him or to look at the picture he'd just finished.

He couldn't see him, couldn't hear him, and a quiet desperation seized him. He needed to remember every detail of every moment he'd had with his son.

Feeling hot moisture behind his eyes, Joe pressed his fists against his face until the dampness disappeared.

When he looked up, his gaze fell on the closet doors. He remembered the sweatshirt Lisa had been studying when he'd come out of the shower. With a sudden need to see his son's artwork again, Joe was at the closet door in two long strides and had his hand in Lisa's suitcase before he could even think about what he was doing.

When he pulled out Cody's shirt, the small package Lisa had wrapped in it fell to the floor with a soft clink. Eager to see Cody's artwork, Joe ignored the package.

Placing the shirt on the bed, Joe smoothed it out with one hand and remembered how incredibly motivated Lisa had been to do whatever she could to encourage their son with his creative streak.

What did you *ever do?*

Joe shoved the awful thought away and fell to his

knees, tracing his finger over the whale his little boy had drawn. He squeezed his eyes shut and swallowed hard. When he opened them again, he ran his hand over the replication of the sea floor and the black and white whale swimming above it. So much detail for such a little guy. Why hadn't he encouraged him more? He could have spent more time with his son. Now he'd never get another chance.

"Cody," Joe whispered. "Buddy, I'm sorry." He buried his face in the shirt, drinking in the little boy scent lingering there.

In that instant, Joe could picture his son happy and smiling. He could even hear the enthusiasm in Cody's voice whenever he'd talk about their upcoming trip.

Without even thinking about it, Joe returned to the closet and grabbed Lisa's sweatshirt. The one that matched Cody's. It, too, held a faint but unmistakable scent. Citrus. He rubbed it against his cheek.

Lisa. Cody. The two people he loved most in the world. He'd let them down. He couldn't undo it, but he could go to Lisa now. He knew her. The shirt with Cody's artwork meant the world to her. If he'd have agreed to go with her, she probably would have suggested taking Cody's shirt so they could feel close to him while they watched the whales.

"Please, Lord, don't let me be too late." Joe grabbed Cody's sweatshirt off the bed and was out the door and halfway to the elevator when he realized what he'd just done. Had he really acknowledged God as if He was right here with him?

Admitting God was present was tantamount to acknowledging his own shortcomings as a father. Joe didn't want to believe it. He didn't want to face the truth. It was far easier to tell himself God abandoned him when He let Cody die, didn't care about him, that He never cared about him.

But if he convinced himself of this then he didn't deserve God's love and the privilege of praying after the way he'd let God down. He'd been entrusted with two lives: Cody and Lisa's. And look what a mess that had become.

The revelation of what he was doing—talking to God, and the acknowledgment of what he'd been doing—denying the Lord because of his own guilt, nearly drove him to his knees. If he'd been in his room instead of an open corridor full of people, that's exactly what he would have done.

Could he really let his guilt outweigh what he knew of the Lord? He didn't want to anymore. But he wasn't sure he was strong enough not to fall back into it. He didn't have to be. Suddenly he wanted to see Lisa. If he shared this with her, she would be his strength and support. She would help him through it.

Like he helped her? The guilt tore at him. How could he expect something from her when he hadn't given her the same thing when she needed it?

Well, she still needed it, and he intended to make it up to her, starting right now. He looked down at the shirt in his hand. Renewed determination and heart drove him toward the elevator.

"OK, Lord, if you're there, make sure I get this shirt to Lisa in time."

8

When Lisa reached the fringes of the crowd, one thing became unsettlingly clear. She'd have to fight her way through the crowd to see the whales since she wasn't tall enough to see from this vantage point.

"Excuse me," she said to an overly tall but friendly looking bald man. He smiled and stepped to the right to provide an opening for her.

"Thank you." She returned the smile and made her way toward the rail. But there was still an unbelievable sea of people ahead of her. Just when she thought she was making progress, the crowd let out a collective moan and quickly pushed their way past her.

As she reached the rail, Lisa could see nothing but dense fog. "What? No!" The mist she'd seen earlier had thickened to a gray wall of vapor that now covered the sky, the blue water, and her precious whales.

"Why, Lord? Why did you bring me here, let me find this spot, only to be disappointed? Don't I deserve something good to happen? Especially knowing it will help me feel closer to my son?" Grief buckled her knees.

"Lady, are you OK?" Strong arms caught her as she stumbled then just as quickly righted her.

Lisa looked into the face of the tall bald man she'd seen earlier. "I'm, um, fine. Thank you."

"I don't know. You don't look so good."

"I'm OK, really. Thank you."

"Why don't you sit down over here?" He led her to the stairwell, and she sat on one of the steps. "Are you sure I can't get something for you? Maybe call someone?"

"No." The only person she could think of wouldn't care anyway. She swallowed hard and tried to look perky. "Thank you, though."

Sitting there, on the cold steps, Lisa had the vague thought that she should go back to the room. But she couldn't get up. Rooted to the spot, she clung to the hope that the fog would lift and the whales would still be there. She feared if they were gone, her last link to her son would be gone as well. Absurd, she knew. But logic didn't dictate emotions.

For a few moments today, she'd felt closer to Joe than she had in a long time. Had she only imagined it? Because now, they were further apart than they'd been throughout the past couple of months.

She'd always clung to the hope that as long as she and Joe were still married, things would eventually work out. Now she wasn't so sure. And even if he finally did come home, things between them would never go back to the way they were, no matter how much she wanted them to.

Eventually she went back to stand at the rail, but when the fog lifted, the whales were gone—and they had taken her hope with them.

This pain would never diminish, not hers and not Joe's. They would never reconcile. Why hadn't she seen before that it would never happen?

All the hope, all the enthusiasm, dissipated from her soul.

The pain…how much longer could she endure it?

The fog rolled back in, and, when the rain began to fall, so did her tears.

****

When Joe stepped off the elevator on the Skygazer deck, the salt air tickled his nose, filling him with hope and anticipation. He searched for Lisa, but she wasn't in the immediate vicinity. In fact, there weren't many people around at all. The twinge of disappointment surprised him. How could the mere thought of seeing the whales with Lisa evoke feelings he didn't think he'd ever feel again?

Is it You, Lord? Are You here with me?

While hope tried to break through, those cynical thoughts of God abandoning him crept back in. It sickened him as he realized he'd spent a good amount of the last several months feeling forsaken. It would be hard work to keep those kinds of destructive thoughts at bay.

As Joe approached the ship's rail, he noticed the deck was wet. It had been raining. No wonder there was such a lack of people milling about the large deck. The color of dirty gray snow, fog blanketed the water and filled the sky. In some spots though, it seemed the sun tried to shine through. Joe squinted against the brightness, knowing he'd missed the whales. If there were whales to be seen, they were hidden in the thickness.

Immediate sadness stung his heart. In his disappointment, he found himself hoping Lisa had been able to see them. He didn't know which disappointed him more. Not seeing the whales at all or not seeing them with Lisa. Perhaps—he looked down at the shirt he held in his left hand—it was not being able to offer her this token and to see her face when he said, "I understand."

Could he really say those words to her and face the hope he'd see in her eyes? He wasn't sure. But just the fact that he was thinking about this proved the Lord was still working in him, *really* working in him. So what was he going to do about it?

Baffled by the depths of his feelings, Joe realized he had a lot of truths to face about himself. For Lisa's sake, he needed to do it now.

Stopping to look around, Joe realized he'd circled the entire deck and hadn't yet seen her. She was nowhere in sight. They'd probably passed each other and hadn't even realized it. He headed to the cabin, hoping she'd gone back there.

Half an hour after Joe arrived back at the cabin, Lisa still hadn't shown up. He'd paced the floor more times than he could count.

Darkness was descending, and the temperature would drop.

Wherever she was, Lisa had to be freezing. What if she'd fallen overboard?

Oh, dear Lord, no. The thought made him feel ill.

Unable to sit and wait, Joe left the cabin and headed back toward the elevator.

He deliberated whether or not he should find one of the stewards. Or he could pull one of the panic alarms. No. He'd find a steward first. Maybe something happened to her and the ship's crew knew about it. They probably tried to notify him while he was out looking for her.

Never one to panic, Joe realized he was doing just that, and it came close to knocking him for a loop.

The elevator arrived with a ding and opened with a quiet swoosh. Joe stepped forward, and a young boy with tousled sandy colored hair rushed past him to smash the buttons on the elevator panel then turned to Joe. "We're going up."

"Brandon, calm down."

"But we have to hurry, Dad. She's 'consolable."

"You mean inconsolable?"

"Yeah. I heard Mom say that one time. She told me it means when you're so sad your heart might break. I hope her heart doesn't break, Dad."

Anxiously, the boy slapped at the buttons again.

"Brandon, settle down, son." The man offered Joe a smile as if to apologize for his son's behavior.

Joe's heart gave a little squeeze. Had he ever acted embarrassed by something Cody did or said? He didn't think so, but suddenly he couldn't be sure. How he wished he could remember every minute he'd ever had with his son.

"Come on. Come on. *Come on!*" Brandon poked at the buttons again.

Brandon's dad aimed another longsuffering sigh in Joe's direction, before he reached down and took his son by the hand. Brandon shrugged out of his father's grip.

"Daa-ad. The lady. We have to hurry. I think she's sad cuz she missed the whales."

Joe tensed. Were they talking about Lisa?

"She kept saying a little boy's name, over and over."

"Cody," Joe murmured. Some of his panic ebbed. Lisa was safe. Upset but safe.

The little boy, Brandon, turned and looked up at Joe.

"Do you know Cody, too?"

Joe swallowed hard and gave a curt nod. "Where is she?"

"The lady?"

"Yes." Joe knew he sounded impatient.

"Her name's Miss Lisa." Brandon sounded almost defiant.

"Brandon, be polite," his dad corrected.

"Sorry, mister." Brandon looked down at the ground.

"It's OK, Brandon. Lisa's my wife, and I've been looking for her for a couple of hours."

"I know right where she is." Brandon straightened and puffed his chest out. "Me and my dad, we're on our way to rescue her."

"Rescue her?"

"Like I told my dad, she's 'consolable. She needs someone to rescue her."

"Show me where she is, and I'll be forever grateful." Joe meant it. "I'll rescue her."

****

They took a couple of wrong turns as Brandon forgot which direction he needed to go, and Joe struggled to stay patient with the little guy. When Brandon finally, proudly, led them to her, Lisa was sitting at the bottom of a cement staircase looking like a lost child. Her bleak, stark expression tore at his heart. He knelt at her side, hoping to offer her some kind of comfort.

"Lisa."

"Joe?" She lifted her head. Her wide blue eyes looked so lost, so shattered. His heart nearly broke.

"Come here." Reaching for her, he spoke as softly as possible. She needed a gentle comfort he didn't think he could offer, but she was his wife, and he intended to try.

The thought came from out of nowhere, startling him, almost stealing his breath. *His wife.* He'd also uttered those words to Brandon just a few minutes ago. Lisa was his wife, and she needed him.

She'd needed him before…when Cody died. She'd needed him more back then than she ever had, and probably ever would. But he couldn't deal with her grief and guilt coupled with his grief and his guilt. The weight of all those negative feelings had overwhelmed him. He'd abandoned her when she needed him most, and he hated himself for it.

Now was his chance to make up for it. But if he did, she could mistake his intentions and think he was coming home. He couldn't do that to her. Not while he was still broken. He would end up hurting her more. For a moment, his insides twisted. But then something bigger overruled that fear and almost brought him to his knees.

He couldn't—*wouldn't*—fail her a second time.

"Come here, Lisa," he said again.

She looked at him with those sorrow-filled eyes and went into his arms with no resistance at all. He gathered her close, tightening his arms around her. He could feel her ribs, and he loosened his touch, afraid she might break.

Too many months had passed since he last held his wife in his arms. As she snuggled closer to him, Joe squeezed his eyes shut.

"Hey." He spoke softly, all the while hardening his mind against thoughts of warmth and comfort. "Do you want to talk about it?"

She began to sob. Heart-wrenching sobs. Sobs that made his gut ache and left him feeling helpless.

Her sorrow wasn't just because she didn't see the whales. He understood the whales were a link between her and Cody. She loved them; Cody loved them. They were something the two of them enjoyed learning about together. For Lisa to see them in the ocean, when Cody always wanted to and never did, was a reminder of their little boy and the joy they would have shared together.

He didn't understand the connection between mothers and sons. Mothers were far more emotional than fathers. But he did understand what he'd missed by always being so busy with work that he sacrificed the father-son connection. He'd have to find a way to tell Lisa he finally understood. But he had to do it in such a way she wouldn't get her hopes up and think he was coming home to her.

Oh Lord, I wish I could. I wish there was a way. But he'd messed her life up so terribly, there was just no way. "Please," he whispered through the pain that clogged his throat.

Did he mean it? Or was this merely lip service? Some emotion tugged at his heart, and only then did he realize he'd been praying.

Is it You, Lord? Are You here with me?

He'd been reaching out to God. But he hadn't done that in a long time. Even long before Cody's death.

Lord, You're really working on me, aren't You? The tug came again and this time he recognized the emotion that came with it. Was it possible? Could there be hope after all?

9

Joe sat next to Lisa in the Skygazer's Café, the closest place to get out of the cold. Despair filled his wife's eyes. He'd brought her here when she finally cried out all of her tears. A pot of tea that smelled like cinnamon steeped in front of her, and Joe poured some into a cup. Then he placed her shaking hands on either side in an attempt to warm her up.

The stark white of her face alarmed him, as did the tinge of blue touching her lips.

"What kind of soup would you like?"

She didn't look at him, let alone respond. It tore him up to see her like this.

"Lisa, please say something." He needed to get through to her. She was much too quiet, much too cold. "Drink your tea so you can warm up. Otherwise I'll have to take you to see the ship's doctor."

"Why, Joe?" she asked in a small voice that sounded nothing like her. She let go of the teacup and finally looked at him. "Why doesn't God hear my prayers anymore?"

This was something he couldn't bear. Lisa questioning her faith. She'd always been so strong, so unshakable in her beliefs. He'd been the weak one, the one whose faith crumbled under trials.

"I missed the whales," she whispered between chattering teeth.

"I know." Joe rubbed her cold hands. He needed

to get her warm, comfort her, and take care of her.

"The fog rolled in just as I made it back to the deck. I totally missed them." Her voice broke, and she swallowed hard. "I wanted to see them. For Cody."

"You'll get another chance, sweetheart. There's bound to be more whales."

She shook her head and looked up at him, her heart's brokenness reflected in her gaze. "I don't think so. Did you ever want something so bad, you just knew it wasn't going to happen?"

Yeah. You. Cody. Our family back together again. The one thing he knew would never happen again. Unable to give voice to his thoughts, Joe shook his head. Now wasn't the time to linger on what he couldn't have. Lisa was here now, and she needed him. Silent grief lingered between them until Lisa looked away and finally began to sip her tea.

When she finished, she set down the cup and stood. "Let's go back to the room. I think I need a hot shower."

"Are you sure you don't want some soup first?"

She was much too thin, and the soup would be good for her.

She shook her head. "Joe, thank you for being there for me tonight. I really do appreciate it."

Something inside him warmed at her words. Taking the focus off himself, reaching out, was good. Giving someone else, Lisa, comfort—what would things be like for them today, if he'd done that months ago?

****

"So how did you find me?" Lisa stood on her

tiptoes, staring out the small cabin window into the twilight. When Joe didn't immediately answer, she looked over to where he sat on the edge of his bed. Lips pressed together, he seemed pensive.

Did he already have regrets about taking her in his arms and comforting her? It had been the last thing Lisa expected to happen. So much time had passed since they held each other. It was warm, safe, right. She wanted to stay in his arms forever.

"I thought about what you said about the whales, and I wanted to talk to you about it. When I couldn't find you, I overheard this young boy talking to his father. His name is Brandon. He's six or seven, I think. Younger than Cody."

"I know Brandon."

"You do? Really?"

"I met him earlier in the day." Lisa told Joe how Brandon helped her when she dropped the flowers at the door and then about seeing him again on the deck.

Joe nodded. "He saw you crying and told his dad about it. He was worried about you, Lisa." He paused. "So was I."

It took a moment for her to absorb this. Joe had actually thought about their argument and wanted to talk about it? He'd been worried about her? Dare she get her hopes up?

No. She couldn't take another letdown. She struggled to keep her expression neutral. "I'm glad you found me."

As soon as she spoke, he nodded and turned away.

She couldn't tell if he was regretful, embarrassed, or happy. Not wanting to push him away when they'd made this small step forward, Lisa went to the closet and gathered some things for her shower.

When she walked past the bunk beds toward the bathroom, she spotted her and Cody's orca sweatshirts lying behind Joe on his bed.

"Joe?"

He ducked his head as if embarrassed then glanced at the shirts before looking at her. He took a deep breath. "I found them in the closet. It's what I wanted to talk to you about."

"You searched my bags? Why?" It was so unlike Joe, she wasn't sure what to say.

"I saw them when you were looking at them in the closet. When you left the room after our argument, I—I needed to see them again."

His voice grew husky.

An ache settled deep in her heart.

"I—I thought about him. About Cody." Joe squeezed his eyes shut, and the sting of tears gathered in Lisa's own eyes. "I tried to picture him happy, smiling. I couldn't. But when I took the shirt out of the closet, looked at his artwork again, I could picture him drawing and could finally imagine him smiling."

He opened his pain-filled eyes and swallowed hard. "I knew you'd want his shirt with you when you saw the whales, so I was bringing it to you," he said, his voice a raw whisper.

"Oh, Joe. Thank you." She turned away and ran into the bathroom so he wouldn't see the tears she could no longer hold at bay.

The hot water washed over her, but that wasn't what eventually seeped through the chill to warm her flesh and bones. It was Him. God. He'd been listening after all. He really was here with her...and with Joe.

"Lord, I'm so confused," she prayed as she stood

under the hot spray. "I thought you didn't hear me any longer. But you did. You sent Joe to find me when I needed him the most."

As she prayed a prayer of thanksgiving and asked forgiveness for her doubts, Lisa began to hope again.

****

While Lisa showered, Joe sat in one of the uncomfortable green chairs holding Cody's whale sweatshirt and tried to figure out exactly what he was feeling.

In some ways, things felt right—not as in 'all is well with the world,' because without their son, the world would never be the same again. But he knew he needed to be here, on this ship, with Lisa, helping her through her heartache.

Then there were these warm feelings still lingering inside him. They both confused and amazed him. Much as he wanted to deny it, he wasn't ready for the feelings to dissipate. What could he do to hang on to them?

"Joe? I think there's someone at the door."

Joe looked up to see Lisa peeking out the bathroom door, face flushed and a towel wrapped around her damp body. He stared a minute too long. Embarrassed, he looked away. Then he almost looked again. Why should he be embarrassed? She was his wife, after all.

Because, you idiot, you abandoned her when she needed you most.

"Joe?" Eyebrows raised along with her voice, Lisa tilted her head toward the cabin door. "The door?"

Only then did he become aware of the knocking

sound.

"Sorry." Disconcerted by his thoughts, Joe tossed Cody's shirt in the other chair before he headed toward the door. Who could possibly be knocking on the door at this time of night, especially on a cruise ship where they didn't know a soul?

An elderly woman stood at the door.

"You must have the wrong room," Joe said.

"Not if you're Lisa's husband, I don't." The woman spoke in a cheerful tone. Too cheerful for what he and Lisa had been through this evening.

"Oh." Joe blinked. He looked back toward Lisa, but she'd disappeared back into the bathroom. When had she made friends? First little Brandon and now this white-haired lady.

"So, are you?" She stared at him, her eyes magnified behind thick glasses.

"Am I what?"

She just smiled and stared some more.

"Oh. Lisa's husband. Yes. I am. Forgive my manners." He held out his hand. "Joe Kendall. And you are?"

"I'm Jessica Lane." She took his hand firmly in hers then covered it with her other one in a comforting manner. She had an unusually strong grip. Though lined with age, her hands were deeply tanned and muscular. She'd obviously worked hard her entire life. "I just heard what happened. Poor Lisa. I wanted to check in on her before I retire for the night. Is she all right? She could have caught pneumonia."

People were talking about Lisa? Just exactly what were they saying? And *who* would be saying anything at all? Lisa didn't know anyone on the cruise. Except, apparently, Brandon and this woman standing here.

"Are *you* all right?"

With a start, Joe realized he was staring at the poor woman as if she had two heads.

"I'm sorry. I just didn't know Lisa knew anyone on the ship."

"We met on one of the upper decks after I saw her in the gift shop. We sat and had a nice long talk. She's a real sweetheart."

Jessica sounded so genuine that Joe couldn't help but smile. "Yes," he agreed. "She is, and she's doing fine. She's taking a shower. When she's finished, I'm going to try to get her to eat some soup."

"She could do with more than soup. She's much too thin."

Joe's sentiments exactly. He nodded. "But I'll be happy just to get some soup in her."

Jessica raised one white eyebrow and looked past his shoulder as though she expected to be invited in. He couldn't very well shut the door in her face, but he didn't want her to see the bunk beds and get too inquisitive.

"I'd invite you in, but Lisa's showering."

"Then why don't I accompany you to the café on the Skygazer Deck while you buy Lisa that soup you mentioned? We can talk along the way."

How could he say no to that? Besides, he was curious to find out exactly what Jessica knew about his and Lisa's relationship. "Let me just get my wallet."

Joe ducked back inside the cabin, inhaling a waft of citrus-scented air that had escaped under the bathroom door. He grabbed his wallet off the nightstand and headed back toward the door, stopping at the sight of Cody's shirt where he'd carelessly tossed it. He scooped it up and spread it across Lisa's bed.

After running his hand over it to smooth out the wrinkles, he knocked on the bathroom door. "Lisa, I'll be back in just a bit."

"Oh...OK, Joe."

If he told her he intended to bring her back something to eat, she'd probably ask him not to leave. So, he left it at that.

****

Joe stepped into the corridor and was met by Jessica, who wore a none-too-friendly scowl. He probably shouldn't have shut the door in her face. "Sorry." He muttered an apology and started down the hall with Lisa's newfound friend.

"I'm worried about Lisa." Jessica tossed the words over her shoulder as she power-walked toward the elevator.

Did she know Lisa well enough to be worried about her? Now Joe was even more curious about this woman.

"I'm worried, too." Joe increased his stride so he could catch up with her. This was no frail little lady fading into the twilight years. He had a feeling she was full of surprises.

"Brandon's father told me she was inconsolable."

So Jessica knew Brandon and his father. This ship was beginning to seem like a small community. The thought made him a little more than uncomfortable.

"Yes," Joe admitted. "Lisa was heartbroken. It kind of scared me. I haven't seen her cry like that in a long time."

Or heard her cry, he amended to himself. This cruise was the first time he'd physically seen her in weeks. But her voice on the messages she left every day didn't sound like someone who'd been crying. Come to think of it, he couldn't remember when he'd last heard her voice on the phone and even *thought* she'd been crying. When had she stopped?

"Why do you think she's so upset?"

Why did it even matter to this woman? Still, she'd sought them out to check on Lisa. "She missed seeing the whales. It has something to do with our son. He loved whales so much."

"So seeing them was important to her. But important enough to cause this kind of response?"

Maybe Jessica was a retired psychiatrist. She was beginning to ask him way too many questions. "No. This is more like she's given up, and I can't stand the thought." Joe scrubbed his hands over his face. "Even when we lost Cody, her faith kept her from giving in to the overwhelming grief. I'm not saying she didn't grieve. She did. She cried a lot. But she didn't let it take her to some dark place she could never come back from."

"What about you?"

Joe shook his head. What was this woman driving at? "Me?"

"Your faith. How did it help you get through?"

That dark place he spoke of…Joe knew it well, and he couldn't believe he was about to share his next statement with a stranger. "It didn't."

She smiled at him, nodded, and didn't say anything.

And her silence somehow built a bridge between him and Jessica. "To tell you the truth, I was kind of relieved when Lisa finally stopped crying over our son."

"Relieved?" Jessica stared at him, much the way he'd stared at her when she'd first come to the cabin.

"Yeah. I know it was selfish on my part." Joe looked away from her unwavering, disbelieving gaze. "I get uncomfortable around a lot of crying, and I was having a hard time with my own emotions. But this..." He waved his hand helplessly. "This hopelessness is so different. I don't know what to do."

Jessica pressed her lips together and nodded. "Hmm." That small sound was ripe with meaning, leaving Joe to wonder what she was thinking.

He almost asked her, but they reached the Skygazer Café, and Jessica hurried inside and up to the counter while Joe was caught holding the door for several smiling and laughing passengers.

Jessica ordered two cups of Earl Grey tea and a bowl of potato soup to go. Joe made it to the counter just as she was fishing in her purse. He quickly pulled out his wallet and handed the waiter the special credit card the ship gave each passenger when they boarded. Call him old-fashioned, but he couldn't let Jessica pay for his tea and Lisa's soup with her ship's credit card. It just didn't feel right.

He carried the tray to a nearby table while Jessica grabbed napkins, some blue packets of sweetener, and stir-sticks.

"Lisa didn't tell me you were so handsome."

A twinge of regret brushed Joe's heart. Did Lisa still even think of him that way? After all he'd put her through? Not that he'd expect her to say so to a total stranger.

"She tells me you don't really want her here."

Oh, great. She apparently knew so much about him and Lisa; it probably wouldn't have mattered if she'd seen the bunk beds.

"What else did she say?"

"Not much else."

"Good," he said wryly.

Jessica looked at him with one eyebrow raised above her glasses. "I don't know whether to be hurt or offended."

"Neither. I'm sorry. I didn't mean to be so rude."

"I understand." She smiled at him, and Joe relaxed just a bit. "We did find out that not only are we neighbors on the Denali Deck, but that we have little Brandon in common,"

Joe nodded. "I'm glad she met both of you." He wasn't sure what else to say so he sipped his tea.

Jessica followed suit, then leaned forward with her elbows on the table. "She did tell me about your little boy." She reached out and squeezed his hand.

Pulling his hand from hers, he turned away so she wouldn't see the moisture gathering in his eyes. Only after he felt like he was finally composed, did he turn back to Jessica.

"I'm sorry," he said.

"No. I'm the one who's sorry. I shouldn't have said that." She pressed her lips together and glanced down at her lap as if embarrassed.

"It's all right, Jessica. Really. That's actually why I'm here."

"Because you lost your little guy?"

"Because my work is suffering, and my boss forced me to take time off or be fired." Never really one to open up to people, Joe marveled that he felt comfortable enough with Jessica to confide in her when he never confided in anyone else.

"What made you decide on the cruise as a way to

spend your time off?"

He shrugged. He might as well tell her. "Because Lisa called and left a message on my voice mail, every single day, telling me I need to deal with my feelings and that I should take the cruise. I guess she thought it would help."

"So why do you think she's given up now instead of then?"

"I honestly don't know."

"You know she blames herself for the accident, don't you?"

"She told you that?" Why would Lisa blame herself? *Perhaps for the same reason you blame yourself.* The small thought whispered through his mind, and he quickly shoved it away.

"Don't worry," Jessica assured him. "She didn't say that to me. But it's a natural thing for a mother to blame herself. And it's apparent that she's not the only one feeling the same blame."

Joe didn't respond. Why on earth did Lisa blame herself? *He* was the one at fault.

"Did you ever stop to think Lisa's doing the very thing she's accused you of? Not dealing with her feelings? Lisa probably called you every day because it gave her something to focus on besides herself."

"You mean worrying about me instead of dealing with Cody?"

Jessica nodded. "I doubt she's dealt with her grief, except marginally. She probably compartmentalized it in such a way that she convinced herself she'd deal with it once you were better. You said she always seemed so strong. Maybe she thought she had to be strong for you and decided she'd deal with her feelings later. Then when she missed seeing the whales, everything just overwhelmed her. All those repressed feelings came rushing to the surface."

Who is *this woman?* Joe shot Jessica a pointed look. But she kept talking as if the look he gave her was perfectly ordinary.

"Something about missing those whales was like a sign to her that not only is Cody really gone, but so are you. You're completely right when you say she's given up."

"What are you, Jessica? A psychologist?"

Jessica flashed him an endearing smile.

"I'm just someone who cares, Joe."

Why? Why *did* she care?

Furthermore, why was he even listening to her? He'd dismissed everything anyone had ever tried to tell him about grieving and finding closure, about Lisa. So why, when he wouldn't listen to those closest to him, was he listening to a stranger? She was a kind and caring stranger with a sympathetic ear and a smile that warmed his heart.

That really wasn't the point. He was at a loss, but one thing he did know.

"You, Jessica, are the answer to a prayer."

"Yours or Lisa's?"

Good question. At this point, he wasn't sure. "Maybe both."

"Maybe," she agreed. "But if you really want to help Lisa, you need to put your heart aside and do something to help pull her out of her slump. I think it might be the only way she'll survive this."

Joe took a big gulp of tea and shut his eyes as he swallowed. He could tell by the glint in Jessica's eyes, this conversation was about to get way too intense.

10

Lisa was disappointed to find the room still empty. She had hoped they could spend some more time talking. She feared if they didn't, this fragile opening they'd found would disappear. Maybe it already had. Could be their talk have scared him off. He'd probably sought out the captain again, hoping an empty cabin might have miraculously appeared.

Heavyhearted, Lisa tiptoed up the ladder to her bed. Cody's sweatshirt was spread out on her pillow. *Joe.* A catch tugged at her heart. He really did care. Much as he concealed it, he did.

She smiled to herself and pulled the shirt close as she climbed under the covers, once again inhaling the little-boy scent that clung to the clothing. Had Joe noticed the scent when he held the shirt? Lisa's throat tightened to an overwhelming ache and the sting of tears burned the backs of her eyes as she remembered the pain etched on Joe's face while he held Cody's shirt and told her how he could actually picture their son—something he hadn't been able to do since Cody died.

"Oh, Joe," she whispered. "Does this mean you're finally able to deal with our loss?"

God really was working in Joe's heart. If she wasn't sure before, she was sure now. She brushed at her tears then began to pray. "You really are here with Joe, Lord. Thank You so much for hearing my prayer. I know You'll help him find a way to deal with his feelings. I pray he'll be open to You and recognize You're always with him. And Lord, thank You that he opened up to me, even if it was just the tiniest bit. I pray he'll talk to me about it some more. Please don't let him shut back down. Wherever he is right now, Lord, please let him come back to me."

After wiping away more tears, Lisa fluffed her pillow and turned to face the door. Why, after all of these months, were the tears she'd struggled so hard to contain suddenly falling so freely? The emotion of the day left her exhausted and struggling to keep her eyes open as she waited for Joe to return.

****

Almost an hour after Joe headed toward the café with Jessica, he'd learned all about her tulip farm in Skagit Valley. He felt envious of the simple, but hard-working life she'd shared with her husband. He walked Jessica to her cabin before heading back to his own with a container of potato soup for Lisa and a head full of advice.

He went back over their conversation. Was Jessica an answer to a prayer? Joe couldn't recall ever being so open with anyone other than Lisa, and after his short time with Jessica, he could almost see things from a different perspective. Something had shifted inside him.

Earlier that evening, it even seemed as though God might be with him. He sensed the reason was that he'd stopped to take his eyes off his own misery for five minutes and finally saw, *really* saw, the hurt his wife was feeling. Or it could be due to Jessica's prodding. Whatever the reason, Joe knew one thing above all else. Lisa was in crisis-mode. Determined to be there for her now, he fumbled with the door key in one hand and the potato soup in the other. As he did, one thought overwhelmed him. He still loved his wife, and he was no longer overcome with the intense, desperate need for her to leave him alone.

After setting the soup on the small table, Joe looked over at the bed where Lisa lay sleeping. Unsure whether he should wake her, he gently whispered her name. Her eyelashes fluttered, but she didn't open her eyes.

It was just as well. Joe watched her for a minute, thinking sleep was probably better than soup right now. Especially if she was able to rest peacefully.

Except Lisa wasn't resting peacefully. He'd watched her sleep so many times through the years he knew she wasn't really sleeping. She had a certain way of breathing at night. Not a snore, something softer, a rhythmic sound that never failed to match the beats of his heart.

Or maybe the beats of his heart matched her breaths.

"Lisa?" he called her name again, not expecting her to answer. For whatever reason, she wanted him to think she was asleep.

Maybe Jessica was right and she did need something to look forward to. Even as he ran the thought through his mind, his stomach twisted into knots. Still, he forged on.

"I know you're awake. But that's OK. You don't have to talk to me. The ship's first port of call is tomorrow. Ketchikan. We can go if you'd like. Think about it."

She still didn't move a muscle, but that was OK.

He knew she heard him. That's what was important. She heard him and hopefully would look forward to morning.

Not that he looked forward to it himself. He would have at one time, but not anymore. And he didn't really think spending the day touring with Lisa was such a great idea.

If it wasn't for his talk with Jessica, he wouldn't have even made the offer. She'd suggested it as a way to cheer up Lisa.

Joe didn't suspect Jessica's motives. She was a kind woman and only seemed concerned about Lisa's welfare, nothing more. Joe was concerned, too. Otherwise, he wouldn't be going out on this limb. Maybe after going into town, Lisa would feel better. Then he would feel better.

He got into bed, dreading morning. But he'd made the offer; he couldn't call it back.

****

It broke Lisa's heart not to answer when Joe whispered her name, but she couldn't let him know she'd been crying again. He had enough on his heart without worrying about her any further. Just knowing he still cared, that he'd come looking for her, touched the deepest part of her soul.

The invitation to go into Ketchikan brought tears to her eyes. He wanted to spend the day with her. Earlier, that knowledge would have sent shivers of hope straight to her heart. Now, she just wasn't so sure.

For a long time, she lay there wondering if it meant they could finally find a way to comfort each other. Were her prayers being answered bit-by-bit?

Listening to him breathe softly on the bunk below her, Lisa realized she'd have to think about it in the morning. Right now, her heart weighed too heavy to look forward to anything.

Lucky for Joe he'd been able to fall asleep so quickly. For him to nod off so quickly tonight must mean he was exhausted.

From looking for her.

Lisa brushed away the whisper of guilt and tried to focus her mind on something else. Like prayer. But it did no good. She couldn't concentrate. Sleep would be a long time coming.

The dull, hollow ache in her chest never seemed to go away, but tonight, her heart ached deeper than usual, her memories of Cody more intense.

Tears seemed to always simmer at the back of her eyes. She could only pray that time would ease the ache and soothe the sting of emotions.

Sometimes, though, she was afraid to pray because God might answer her prayer and lessen her pain. But would that mean she'd forget her son?

No! A sob tore from her before she could stop it. She buried her face in her pillow, not wanting to disturb Joe.

Too late, she heard Joe's covers rustling, followed by his footsteps on the floor.

A second later his breath whispered across her neck, the touch of his hand tucking her hair behind her ear, gently touching the exposed part of her cheek just above her jawline.

"Lisa?"

She grew still, her face buried in her pillow, and tried to keep herself from revealing she was awake.

"Come on, Lisa. I know you're awake." His deep voice rumbled in her ear, and she realized he was standing on the ladder to her bunk. She held her breath, her pride too strong to let him see her tears or to share with him just how deeply she hurt.

He gave a none-too-gentle tug on the edge of her pillow. "You're going to suffocate in that pillow, you know."

The depth of caring she heard in his voice warmed her heart. For so long, he'd scarcely acknowledged her. Compelled to ease some of the worry she heard in his voice, she finally answered him. "I'm not going to suffocate, Joe. I'm awake. I'm fine. Now go away."

After all the agonizing over his remoteness, and the hope and prayers for them to be able to comfort each other, why in the world was she telling him to leave her now?

She hadn't planned for Joe to see her cry anymore; she was certain that's what had driven him away in the first place.

If only he knew how much guilt she had stored in her heart.

****

Oddly disappointed by Lisa's refusal to let him comfort her, Joe settled back into bed and closed his eyes. But his mind wouldn't settle. Frustrated, Joe recognized the sharp sting of rejection. All he wanted to do was comfort her, help her out of this dark place she'd found herself at tonight.

Like she tried to do so often for you.

Now he knew exactly how she felt when he refused to let her in. *Lisa, what are we going to do?* He wished he could go back to ignoring her, but he couldn't. Neither could he go back to that dark place where he shut everything, and everyone, out.

Ashamed of himself, of the way he'd abandoned Lisa, Joe knew he couldn't leave Lisa to deal with this hopelessness by herself. He needed to be there for her in ways he hadn't been before. He couldn't abandon her a second time.

The enormity of his failure staggered him. She deserved better than to have him in her life. Then a new thought flickered at the edges of his mind. Even though he thought it was best for her, could it be possible the divorce would only bring more pain and devastation to Lisa?

Are you listening, Lord? I'm so confused. How can I help her without hurting her more?

He might be confused about what was best for Lisa, but he did know one thing. While she'd come here intending to help him, he was about to turn the tables and help her. Tomorrow morning when they woke up, Lisa would find him with a different attitude.

****

Joe's heart caught. Clearly, Lisa hadn't slept well. Traces of the despair and desolation from last night still showed in the dark smudges under her eyes that showed through her cosmetics.

He would give anything to wipe the sorrow from her eyes.

"Good morning."

She jumped, clearly not expecting to see him already up and dressed for the day.

"I've been waiting for you," he said.

"You have?"

Joe could almost convince himself that something in her voice perked up, and he wished he could call back his words. He didn't want to give her false hope. But he couldn't seem to help himself. Feeling almost desperate to find a way to help her over the disappointment of not seeing the whales, Joe forged ahead. "Jessica invited us to eat breakfast with her in the dining room. I wanted to know if you'd like to go."

"No, I don't think so."

"No?" He didn't believe she meant it even as she shook her head.

"Aren't you hungry?"

"Not really."

"OK, then." Joe tried not to focus in on the fact that she'd missed dinner last night. Instead, he made the offer she'd ignored last night. Another of Jessica's suggestions, but Lisa didn't need to know. "The ship's first port of call today. Ketchikan. Would you like to go?"

"No."

Lisa's negative answers frustrated him, but why was it suddenly so important to him that she agree to do something today? "You want to just sit around here all day?"

"I think so."

"Isn't that what you didn't want me to do? You said it wasn't good for me."

"Maybe I was wrong. Maybe you were right to sit around all day doing nothing."

Joe sighed, at a momentary loss over what to do. He had to save Lisa from spiraling into the same deep, dark despair he'd allowed himself to cultivate. If she lost sight of God, as he'd done, she would have nothing to draw from in a crisis.

But Lisa wasn't like him, he reminded himself. Lisa had faith; she had strength. She just seemed to have forgotten for the moment. He had to point her in the right direction.

"OK. The dining room is out. Going into town is out. There's a solarium down the hall from us. It has an enclosed balcony, comfortable chairs, and a beautiful view. How about if I go get us some breakfast? We can take it down there and eat while we watch the view."

"I said I'm not hungry."

Before Joe could respond, Lisa ran into the bathroom, slamming the door behind her.

Tension crept up his shoulders and he rolled them backward in an attempt to loosen them up. More frustrated with himself than her, Joe paced the room. Why had he pushed this on her the very second she woke up? He should have waited until she'd been awake awhile before he said anything.

The way their roles had reversed in the course of one day struck him as ironic.

While he paced, he tried to focus on how he might get through to Lisa. *Please, Lord, what can I do?* As he prayed, he stopped to stare out the window. It wasn't quite sunrise, but the view was astonishing. Calming. Humbling.

Beyond the nearby islands, far in the distance, a snow-covered mountain towered against the deep purple backdrop of the sky. White mist draped across the majestic peak illuminated in varying shades of pink and orange by the sun as it began to rise.

A hush came over him, and it was as though God stood right there with him.

Lisa had to see this. If it spoke to her as powerfully

as it did to him, well...it might make a difference. It might even bring a smile to her face.

She chose that moment to come back into the room.

He took a deep breath and started to speak, but his instinct tried to take over and take him back to yesterday when all he thought about was himself and his misery. But it wasn't about him anymore. It was about Lisa. And listening to the Lord.

Taking another breath, he said something he never imagined he'd say. "I miss you, Lisa. Having you here, I—I didn't realize how much."

She stood in front of him, staring at the floor. He wasn't even sure she even listened. He hoped so, because there was something else that had to be said. Joe's heart hammered out his fear, but he spoke anyway. "I'm sorry I treated you so badly yesterday and the day before. I'm sorry for a lot of things. I was hoping we could talk. You were right when you said it would be good for me to get out and see something besides these walls. Sitting around hasn't been good for me, and I don't think it'll be good for you, either."

She looked at him then, really looked at him. At least that was the way it seemed. But she didn't answer, and his disappointment squeezed his heart.

"Come here." He held his hand out to her. "I want to show you something."

****

Lisa's bruised heart warmed just a bit as she watched Joe as he stood at the tiny window, a shadow of a smile playing on his face. She'd waited months to see him smile again.

Uncertain, she took a step toward him and stopped. He was just being nice to her because she'd been so upset last night. It meant nothing. She shouldn't read anything into it. Nothing.

"Come on, Lisa."

She reached toward his outstretched hand, eager for his touch. As her hand found his, she closed her eyes and reveled in the warmth of his skin against hers. Then he took a sharp breath. She looked at him, searching the depth of his brown eyes. They gave nothing away.

Still holding her hand, he nodded toward the window. What could he possibly want her to see at this hour? It was too dark to see anything.

The whales. It came to her in a flash. They must be out there. That was the reason for Joe's partial smile.

Stepping up on her tiptoes, she peered out the window. No whales were in sight, but she still inhaled in appreciation as her eyes soaked in the wondrous beauty in front of her.

God's promise. He was here. She could see Him all around her, could *feel* Him whisper through her heart. He created this special dawn just for her. To show her He reigns. He is. He loves. He cares. She knew it. Even in those horrific moments when Cody died, she knew the Lord loved her and was with her. And she believed it. But from that moment until now—she hadn't *felt* it. She'd been as empty as Joe.

Now, looking out the tiny window, her heart filled with the wonder her mind had known all along. Her heart burned with it, rejoiced in it. This glorious sight was the Lord's way of saying, "I'm here."

Her God, her shelter. He thought of her. In this great big world filled with billions of people, *He* thought of *her*. Empty as she'd been, as low as she'd been, He hadn't left her.

Had He not shown her this before because she wasn't ready for the message? Another reason could be that while she'd been able to draw her strength from Him to get through those awful days, weeks, and months, now she was on the verge of going down the same dark path as Joe and totally withdrawing from everything and everyone.

And Joe. She hoped Joe saw and felt the same thing she did right now.

She had to share these thoughts with Joe. There was something there; she sensed it. But she didn't want to push it.

It took her a minute to soak it all in. "It's beautiful."

"Yes, it is." Now Joe's smile filled his face and her uncertainty began to fade.

"He made it for me." The feeling burst through her, and she couldn't help but practically shout. "Me. It was what I needed. God didn't forget about me. And..." she hesitated, uncertain if she should say it.

"Me?"

"Yes, Joe. You, too."

"I know," he whispered. At that moment, she would have given anything to know his thoughts. But he turned from her and slipped out of the room before Lisa could even see his expression.

11

Uncertain if she should follow Joe or wait, Lisa went back to the window and stared at the breathtaking sunrise. She wasn't sure how much time passed before Joe came back into the room, but the sky was no longer purple and the mist had risen.

"OK." Careful to speak softly, she held her breath and prayed he hadn't changed his mind about wanting to spend time with her. She hesitated before turning to face him.

Joe held two paper cups encased in fancy brown cardboard sleeves. He furrowed his brow, clearly not knowing what she was talking about.

"Here." He hesitated then held out one of the cups. "I brought you some tea."

She took the cup from him, put her nose over the tiny opening in the lid, and inhaled the steamy heat. It smelled wonderful, and a small sigh escaped her before she could call it back.

"It's cinnamon something-or-other. I hope you like it."

"It's perfect. Thank you."

"You said OK. OK, what?"

"I'll eat breakfast with you in the solarium." She took a sip of tea and watched him closely, waiting for him to say something. He seemed to freeze. Maybe he'd changed his mind. Maybe that's why he was gone so long. "If that's still OK with you?" she added quickly.

After a moment, he relaxed his brow and gave her a half-smile. Lisa wished the smile reached the depths of his brown eyes. "Of course it is. I'm glad you changed your mind."

"I hope you aren't too disappointed about Ketchikan. I just don't want to be around a lot of people today." Her heart still felt battered and bruised from the night before. She didn't have what it would take to put on a happy face.

"It's OK. We'll get out of this cramped up cabin, have a relaxing breakfast, and let it be what it is." He walked over and looked out the window.

"The sunrise is gone." Though the purple mist and pink and orange hues of the sunrise faded away, the warmth of God's promise was still there and hope soared through Lisa's heart. "But the view is still beautiful."

"I know." When Joe turned away from the window he seemed more relaxed. "And we'll have a great view from the solarium."

Lisa smiled at him, still basking in the warmth of the Lord ministering to her soul. If Joe hadn't shared it with her, she'd probably still be feeling hopeless.

"Thank you, Joe." She reached out and clasped his hand and caught her breath when, instead of pulling away, his fingers gently curled against hers. She reveled in the warm feelings that invaded her senses.

"What are you thanking me for?"

"For taking care of me last night." She clasped his hand tighter. Relieved when he didn't pull away, she gave him a wary smile. "For showing me a glimpse of heaven this morning. It did something to my heart. I need to spend some quiet time with God so I can understand it better. When I do, I'll share it with you if you're interested. But for now, just thank you for making me feel better."

She gave him a light kiss on the cheek then hurried into the bathroom and leaned against the closed door.

What had she just done?

Though her heart was undoubtedly lighter, it still slammed against her ribs and thundered in her ears. It was one thing to take his hand, but quite another to kiss him. Funny how those natural impulses took over when she was feeling more relaxed around him. Still, she couldn't help but wonder how Joe reacted.

And though she felt it in her heart, it was only when she looked in the mirror that Lisa realized she had a wide smile on her face.

****

Bewildered, Joe sank down into one of the ugly olive chairs and stared at the door that stood between him and Lisa. He touched his cheek where she'd kissed him just now.

What had he gotten himself into?

For one half-second, he wished he could go back to yesterday morning. Dark, brooding, and shutting her out. But he realized he didn't want to be there now. He knew he'd taken his eyes off God, the way Lisa had said, and he didn't want to do so again. When had she become so wise? Even if she thought otherwise, she'd clearly grown spiritually while he'd stayed stagnant. Or, more accurately, he'd slipped backward.

He got up and crossed over to the tiny window, wishing he could have another look at the beautiful dawn Lisa was so certain God put there for her—for them.

Are you here with me, Lord?

Joe wanted Him to be. He wanted a second chance to be a better human being. Too bad Cody couldn't be here for it. He'd never get another chance to be a better father to his son. He'd ruined that forever.

But this might be a chance for him to be a better person for Lisa, to make up for his failures in just the tiniest of ways. Not that he could ever make up for it completely. Ever. But the smile Lisa just flashed him, the kiss on the cheek...Something good was happening in her heart. She said it was because of him taking care of her last night and sharing the dawn this morning. Could it be he was doing something right for once? Or maybe he was simply manipulating her.

He squeezed his eyes shut, wishing he could drown out his conscience.

I want to depend on you, Lord.

If he wasn't careful, if he failed again, this could still end in divorce.

****

As she showered and dressed, Lisa kept thinking of the sound of Joe's voice as he whispered her name last night while she pretended to sleep. That, along with his offer of spending the day with her, sent shivers of hope through her heart.

He still cared. He'd proven it last night when he'd searched for and then took care of her.

Either that or he felt sorry for her. No. Lisa quickly dismissed the thought. He cared and a door had opened. She now had a chance to get through to him. She could picture the two of them back in Seattle, walking off the ship hand-in-hand, heading home to Whidbey Island.

Today, for the first time in a long time, they would be spending time together. Eating, talking, and maybe even laughing. Again, a sense of hope whispered through her. This was so much better than last night when all she could feel was desolation, sorrow, and guilt.

She gave herself a last once over in the mirror and reached for the doorknob.

Please, Lord, bless our day together.

****

Lisa watched as Joe set the tray on the small, round table between two lounge chairs. He was trying so hard to make her comfortable, and it touched her deeply. When he motioned for her to sit, she did. Warmed by the morning sun, the cozy nook in the solarium was a perfect place for intimate conversation.

Not that she and Joe were going to be intimate, but they were together. And alone. They could talk freely. Maybe now, Joe would open up to her a little more.

"This is perfect, Joe. Especially the French toast." She stared at the two food-laden trays Joe had brought to the solarium while she was in the shower. "But I'll never be able to eat all of this."

"I know how you love your carbs, even though you look like you've missed a few here and there. Just eat what you can. I'm sure I can find room for the rest."

She ignored the comment that was clearly directed at her weight. She'd lost weight. So had he, obviously. What parent in their situation wouldn't? She placed a hand on her abdomen. There was more she should tell him. But it wasn't something she could discuss right now. Instead, she turned her attention to the food. "Where did you get all of this?"

"The Kodiak Grill. It's just down the deck from the Skygazer Café and the food is served cafeteria style."

Joe took a healthy bite of a biscuit and egg sandwich, and Lisa was happy to see him enjoy something for a change. Maybe he'd be able to gain back some of the weight he'd lost.

"What?" Joe put his biscuit down and stared back at her.

"Nothing." A glow warmed her insides. Caught off guard, she blinked. She couldn't possibly be feeling happy. Joy was an emotion reserved for the day Joe came home with her.

"Then why are you staring at me?"

"I didn't mean to. It's just hard for me to believe we're actually sitting and eating together. It's been a long time."

Joe looked away from her, out at the water. The ship moved slowly past a forest-covered island.

"There are tons of eagles on the shore over there." He changed the subject deliberately. Lisa could tell. But she was determined not to push things. They were together. For whatever reason, he'd invited her to share a meal with him. She'd take a small bit of delight in it and not push things. So she merely nodded and turned her eyes in the direction he pointed, even though she couldn't see any eagles.

"Hi, kids." Lisa and Joe both turned from the view to see Jessica, appearing winded, but with a smile on her face. "Do you mind if I sit for a minute while I catch my breath?"

"Morning, Jess. Please, sit." Joe pointed to an

empty lounge chair, and Lisa couldn't help but notice the familiar way he'd shortened Jessica's name. Her husband had apparently spent enough time with a stranger to feel familiar giving her a nickname.

Jessica sat in the lounge chair next to her and promptly reached out and squeezed Lisa's hand. "How are you doing today?"

"Much better, Jessica. Thank you. Joe told me you came by last night. I appreciate your thinking about me."

"You're out early." Joe was pleasant, sincere. "Where are you off to in such a hurry?"

"Oh, nowhere in particular. I'm just trying to walk off all the calories I consumed at breakfast. They have great food." She eyed their plates. "It looks like you're eating pretty well, too. Are you enjoying your morning?"

"We are."

Whether he meant it, or was just making small talk with Jessica, Lisa couldn't help but feel happy.

"Hey, are you two going into Ketchikan today?"

"No." Lisa spoke up. "Joe suggested it, but I'd rather stay here. This little solarium is very relaxing, and I have a book I've been anxious to start reading."

A look passed between Jessica and Joe, but it disappeared before Lisa could interpret it.

"OK. But if you feel like visiting later, I should be back around four o'clock." Jessica sounded uncertain. But Lisa couldn't think of a reason why. "We can have tea if you'd like."

"Thanks. I'll think about it, Jessica." Lisa smiled gently. While she'd certainly enjoy visiting with the older woman, she really had her hopes pinned on time spent with Joe. "Have a nice time in Ketchikan."

Jessica started to leave but stopped and turned back around. "Better yet, why don't you two join me for dinner tonight? So far, at every meal, there've been two or three empty spots at our table."

"I don't think—"

"We'd love to join you, Jessica," Joe answered for both of them.

Unable to speak, Lisa could only stare at Joe. Had she somehow landed in an alternate universe? Not that she believed in such things, of course. But he'd just accepted Jessica's invitation for dinner. It had been many years since he'd accepted a dinner invitation without the ulterior motive of winning over a client.

Joe must have interpreted the look she gave him, because he leaned close and whispered in her ear. "It's OK, Lisa."

"Are you sure?"

"I'm sure."

Jessica rocked back on her heels, looking extremely pleased with herself.

"Well then, I'll see you two kids tonight." She gave them directions to the dining room, winked at Lisa, and headed toward the elevator.

"She's looking way too smug."

"I'm sorry, Joe. I may have told her a little too much about our situation. Now it looks like she's trying to fix our life for us. We absolutely do not have to go. I promise I didn't set her up to it."

"Relax. I know you didn't. I probably told her way too much, too."

"You did?"

"Yeah. She kind of has that effect on people."

Lisa couldn't help but laugh. "She does, doesn't she?"

"Anyway, you deserve a nice dinner. Especially after last night."

"I don't want you to be nice to me just because you feel sorry for me because of last night."

"I'm not, Lisa. I'm—I don't know what to say. Let's just go to dinner tonight, and let it be what it is. OK?"

Warm sensations flooded her heart. At the same time, hot tears filled her eyes and a painful lump tightened her throat.

"Please? Lisa?" His touch was gentle as he turned her chin to face him.

"OK." Lisa tried to smile and swallowed hard as she looked up at him. "OK," she said again. Her face felt so right cradled in his hand, she found herself searching his eyes with her own...and she had the strangest feeling he was going to kiss her.

****

When Joe saw the moisture in Lisa's eyes, he leaned closer and cupped her face in both hands. He wanted to comfort her, wipe her tears away, kiss her, hold her close and never let her go.

"Lisa," he murmured.

"Don't look now, but we've got company."

Joe dropped his hand from Lisa's cheek, relieved to be snapped back to reality. He'd almost kissed her. It would have been a disaster.

"Hi, Miss Lisa. Are you still 'consolable?'" Brandon, as enthusiastic as always, stopped directly in front of Lisa, his expression a mixture of joy and concern. His dad followed close behind.

"Brandon. Don't bother them." Brandon's dad's

face was flushed as he came to a stop next to Brandon.

"It's OK." Lisa said cheerfully. "He's not bothering us, really." She paused then took Brandon's hand. "Brandon, I'm feeling much better today. Mostly because you helped Joe find me last night. Thank you." She spoke so gently and soothing, her words tugged directly at Joe's heart.

Brandon beamed as he stared up at Lisa. Apparently, she knew just what to say to tug on the little boy's heart, too.

Her smile was just as bright, though Joe could detect a glimmer of moisture in her eyes. The smile was for Brandon and Brandon alone, even though it took everything within her to smile. The tug at his heart grew stronger, and he wanted to pull her close. Instead, he turned to Brandon's dad.

"I'm Joe Kendall and this is my wife, Lisa. We never did catch your name."

"It's Chad. Chad Cole." The man's scowl lightened somewhat. "And as you already know, this is Brandon. It's nice to meet you both."

Joe extended his hand to Chad, who shook his hand then turned to Lisa. "How are you feeling this morning?" Chad's scowl had totally disappeared, replaced by a vague smile.

Lisa let go of Brandon's hand in order to shake Chad's.

"I'm doing much better, Chad. Thank you." Lisa pulled her hand from his and turned back to the little boy.

"And Brandon, I'm glad to see you again today so I can thank you properly for helping Joe find me last night. You're a real hero."

A rosy blush tinged Brandon's cheeks, and he

looked down at his shoes for just a second before he looked at her again, his smile bright.

"Me and my dad are going to Catch-can. Are you going there, too?"

"Ketchikan," Chad corrected him.

"Thanks, Brandon. But I don't think so." Joe smiled at the boy. "Lisa's still feeling a little tired, so we're just going to stay here and relax today."

"OK." A slight frown formed between Brandon's sandy-colored eyebrows but disappeared as he quickly went on to his next thought. "Did you know this ship's so huge it can't get close to the dock? That's why we're going so slow. Then, when we stop, we get to ride on this really cool-looking boat all the way to shore. I can't wait!" As if to prove his point, he jumped up and down.

"Brandon," his father warned.

In true little-boy style, Brandon ignored his dad. "Did you know they have seaplanes in Catch-can?" His blue eyes grew wide as he said it. "I heard some of the other people talking about it."

"Oh?" Surprisingly, a spark of interest lit Joe. He hadn't looked forward to very much in the last several months, hadn't been interested in anything. But a seaplane flying over the forests and glaciers? He could almost catch some of Brandon's little-boy enthusiasm. "Are you and your dad going to ride on one?"

Too bad Lisa didn't want to go to shore. Not that it mattered. There was no way she'd ever step on to a seaplane. She hated to fly. Period.

"Nah. We're going exploring. Nuthin' special. Maybe see some totem poles, and I think we're going to a salmon bake." Brandon wrinkled his freckled, sunburned nose.

"Well, I hope you and your dad have fun."

"Thanks." Brandon kicked his toe at the carpeted floor of the solarium. "The totem poles might be cool, but I don't think I'll like the salmon. It's fish." He made a face that reminded Joe of Cody when he didn't want to eat something he thought would be gross.

"Don't you like fish?"

"No way!"

"I don't like it either." Lisa's response was quick, and Joe couldn't help but smile because he knew that like Brandon, a salmon bake was the last thing Lisa would want to attend.

"I really wanted to ride on the seaplane, but my dad says it's too 'spensive."

"Let's go, Brandon. We've taken enough of the Kendalls' time." Joe flinched at Chad's sharp tone, which was most likely due to embarrassment at having his son announce to the world they couldn't afford something. Joe might have acted the same way if his son had mentioned their finances—before he'd come face-to-face with the reality that in the big scheme, a child's honesty was something to cherish.

"He's not bothering us, Chad," Lisa said.

"No," Joe agreed. "He can talk with us anytime."

Chad nodded. "We'd better get going, or we'll miss the shuttle boat."

"Have fun with your dad, Brandon." The cheer in Lisa's voice sounded forced, but her face gave no indication of her feelings.

"Bye, Miss Lisa. See you later." The little boy waved before he charged off down the hall, his dad following behind.

Smile firmly in place, Lisa waved back as Brandon and Chad disappeared around the corner. Then her smile was gone now. "He really wants to ride on a seaplane."

"They have some tours scheduled in Juneau tomorrow. Maybe we can sign up for one." Joe couldn't help but hope she'd be willing. "It can be our way to thank Brandon for finding you yesterday."

Lisa's blue eyes grew wide and her mouth dropped open. "No, thank you, Joseph Kendall. You can go, and take Brandon and his father, but I sure won't. You know better than to even suggest such a thing."

"Fine." He sighed. Even though he expected it, her response left him feeling disappointed. "I was just trying to think of something we could do to make his day a little brighter. He's a sweet kid."

"He is," Lisa agreed. Her tone grew quiet. "Little boys need to have fun."

Was she thinking about Cody? Joe found himself wanting to pull her into his arms and comfort her, but didn't. He wasn't sure how far to take this thing. Making her day brighter was one thing, touching her, holding her was quite another.

"I think maybe we should pray for Chad and Brandon to have a good day."

Lisa's declaration caught him off guard, and Joe swallowed hard, thinking of Cody.

Yesterday he would have said God didn't listen to him anymore. He would have said he didn't pray anymore. He couldn't say either of those things because something happened to him yesterday and suddenly prayer once again was an option.

Whether for Brandon and his dad, or for Lisa or himself, rekindling his prayer life was definitely something he needed to think more about.

It wasn't a conversation he wanted to have with Lisa right now, if ever, so Joe simply began gathering up their dishes. "I'll take these back to the Kodiak Grill. Do you want me to bring you anything else?"

"No, thank you. I think I'll just sit here a while and watch the water."

Was she hoping to see the whales again? His sudden overwhelming need to pull her into his arms was unexpected. Ironic he would feel this way, given his past record of offering her comfort. Would it be hypocritical for him to take her into his arms after having neglected her for so long? He took one last look at his wife and then headed toward the elevator.

12

Every instinct within her said Joe wanted to hold her just now. But he'd run.

Lisa paced the solarium floor along the wall of windows that allowed her to view the water. Earlier, before Brandon arrived, Joe had been about to kiss her.

Had he finally realized he still loved her, and that she loved him? Perhaps his offer to come home would be just around the corner.

Instead of driving herself crazy with questions, Lisa headed up to the Skygazer Deck for a brisk walk in the fresh air. Maybe it would help clear her head and give her the answers she needed.

She wished her cell phone had service so she could call and talk to Rose about it, to see if her perception was right. There was always Jessica, of course, except she'd have to wait until Jessica returned from Ketchikan. Lisa smiled at the thought of her new friend. What would Jessica say? She'd probably tell Lisa she should have agreed to go into Ketchikan today.

But going to Ketchikan wouldn't have made a difference. Joe's invitation had been an empty one. He didn't really want to go. Still, he'd made the offer, and she couldn't help but think that he was simply trying to make up for her being so upset last night.

One thing was for certain. Whether he'd wanted to go to Ketchikan or not, he had wanted to kiss her. She didn't really need to confirm her feelings with either Rose or Jessica.

Lisa could kick herself for making him worry about her last night, for showing him her vulnerability. Her perpetual sadness was, of course, the reason he'd stopped coming home. So it seemed odd that after last night he'd want to spend any part of today with her. Still, his concern appeared genuine. Maybe it wasn't an empty invitation after all.

She considered asking him to go to Juneau in the morning. If she did, he would most certainly want to ride in the seaplane. His interest in that was definitely real. She shuddered, certain she couldn't get on one of those planes. The very thought sent her heart slamming against her ribs.

Then again, she might be able to if putting aside her fear meant she could spend time her husband.

****

When Joe got back to the solarium, Lisa wasn't there. He went to their room and found it empty. He couldn't go through this again. Just as he stepped out the door to go search for her, she came around the corner.

"Where were you?" He winced at the demanding tone in his voice. "Sorry. I was worried. I know you were upset after our conversation with Brandon. I didn't want you to go off by yourself and feel sad again."

"I'm fine, Joe. Really." She gave him a reassuring smile and brushed past him into the room. "I just went for a walk."

"Oh." He really shouldn't be upset, but didn't she

understand he was worried about her after the whale incident?

Lisa sat down in one of the green chairs then looked up at him. "I'm thinking maybe we should have gone into Ketchikan. That way we wouldn't have to spend so much time in this cramped little space."

"Yeah, I'm sorry about that. I don't really know what happened with our room, because we—"

"Cabin." Lisa's smile was wide.

Fifteen minutes ago when Joe left her in the solarium, she looked sad. Now she was smiling.

"Jessica told me it's called a cabin when you're on a ship."

"Right. I wasn't thinking." Joe grinned. "Not about that, anyway. I was thinking about how much we paid for a private balcony. Remember? I don't know where the mix-up was, but I didn't have the energy to question it when I first checked in. And bunk beds? Really?"

Lisa ducked her head, looking suddenly shy.

Great. He was flirting with her. He shouldn't be doing that. He still hadn't sorted out his own feelings.

"There was supposed to be a bed for us and bed for Cody." Lisa was quiet for the space of a heartbeat and when she looked up at him, her smile had faded. "I guess it's a good thing we have the bunk beds, given our current situation."

Joe said nothing.

"I think I'll take my book and go back to the solarium and read for a while." Lisa took the two short steps to the bed and stuck her hand under the pillow.

She withdrew a book. *Just like home.* She probably even had a little flashlight under there. Either that or one of those little lights that clipped on the pages. He found a strange comfort in knowing some things never changed.

When Lisa pulled the sweatshirt with Cody's artwork over her head, a feeling of warmth washed over Joe as he recalled the way seeing it yesterday sparked memories of his son, followed by his subsequent talk with God.

"I think I'll join you." He grabbed his own book off the nightstand and followed her back to the solarium. "At least there, we can watch the view."

He waited until they were both settled in the comfy chairs, and then hesitantly mentioned what he'd hoped to tell her about yesterday. "I told you yesterday that I knew you'd want Cody's shirt when you saw the whales, and that's why I was bringing it to you."

"I remember." Lisa focused her blue eyes on him, watching him intensely. He wanted to hold her gaze, but he looked away.

"Do you remember the rest of what I said?"

"That you tried to picture him happy and smiling. When you looked at his artwork on the shirt, you could picture him that way."

Joe nodded. "When you first told me having the shirt with you helped you to feel close to him, I didn't understand. Ever since he died, I've been having a hard time picturing his face. Then I sat there with the shirt, and I could see him at the table drawing his whales, just chatting away. It was then when I understood why you so desperately needed to see the whales."

Lisa touched him lightly on the arm, and he resisted the urge to crush her to his chest. "I'm glad," she said quietly. "I'm sorry we missed them."

The bittersweet warmth of her tone made his

desire to hold her even stronger. He swallowed hard and looked her in the eye, determined to tell her what was in his heart. Even though it was difficult, even though it made him vulnerable, it was something she needed to know.

"I didn't want you here. I thought you were following me just so you could try to get me to come home."

Lisa looked away from him and stared out at the fishing boats in the water.

"But now I understand." He meant it. "You need to be here to find that closure, too. When I was finally able to picture Cody's face, it was as if someone unlocked a door. I know why you're here. I know why you brought the shirt. And if nothing else comes of this, at least I can visualize our little boy again."

Still staring at the water, Lisa didn't answer.

Had he revealed too much? Part of him knew a great burden had lifted off his shoulders. Another part of him wished he could take it all back.

Feeling awkward, but unwilling to leave her presence, he picked up his book and pretended to read. He should leave, but sitting here with Lisa gave him such an odd sense of comfort. He remembered yesterday when he'd had such a strong feeling that the Lord was here with him. He was here now. And it was He who kept Joe sitting here next to Lisa, no matter how much he believed he should run.

If only He could fill Joe in on what Lisa was thinking. *Please, Lord.*

The prayer whispered through his mind as naturally as if he really had been holding up his end of the relationship with the Lord instead of letting it drop at the same time he'd ignored his family while building his career.

****

Guilt struck deep in her heart, and Lisa hated herself. For more than a moment, really. Long enough for Joe to fall asleep. Still staring out at the water, she heard the soft sound of his book fall. Out of the corner of her eye, she could see it resting on his chest where it had dropped. She reached over and picked it up and then set it on the small table between them.

Had he really been reading, or was it merely a way to avoid any further deep-hearted confessions? He looked so vulnerable, raw, not the least bit peaceful. She watched him for a moment, feeling uncertain. He'd been honest with her. Never a sentimental man, he'd dug into the depths of his being to share those feelings, and Lisa was thankful.

Some healing had happened in Joe's heart, and she could only pray it continued. Unfortunately, it also opened up a quagmire of guilt in her heart. She really shouldn't continue to let him think she was here to find closure. She needed to tell him she really did come on the cruise to try to get him to come home. But if she did, he might get angry and shut down. He was talking to her, and that was such a good sign. They'd made some sort of tenuous progress, and she didn't want to do anything to ruin it. But she feared for what he might do when he learned her real motive for coming aboard. If she didn't correct him now, it would be lying. Rose could tell her all day long that it wasn't, but allowing him to believe something false was the same as if she outright lied. Plain and simple. And Joe not only wouldn't forgive her; he'd probably stay in the next port and figure out some other way to get home.

He'd put himself out there, been honest with her. She needed to do the same for him. If he returned home without knowing the truth, it would be a hollow victory.

Unable to focus on the book, Lisa gave up and tossed it aside. She went to the Skygazer Café and ordered two iced teas. She was thirsty, and Joe would be, too, when he woke up.

He was still sprawled out on the lounge chair when she returned. She stared at him for a minute, aching to reach out and touch him. Having made her decision to be honest with him, she knew this might be the last bit of time he'd spend with her.

Lisa sat in the chair next to Joe's and stared out at the water. Waiting for him to wake up, she tried to summon courage and words.

"Hey." Joe's voice startled her out of her thoughts. "You look upset. What are you thinking about?"

This was it. Lisa took a deep, steadying breath. It would be all right. It had to be. "Joe, I—

A loud noise from the direction of Joe's stomach interrupted her, and he immediately apologized. But a smile quirked the corners of his mouth, and Lisa couldn't help but smile back.

"I guess I slept most of the morning away. Are you ready for some lunch? Do you want to finish talking while we eat?"

It wasn't exactly a mealtime conversation, but Lisa nodded. She would save the confession for later, and in the meantime she'd choke down everything on the menu if it meant spending one more afternoon with Joe.

****

As they sat in the Kodiak Grill eating lunch, Lisa wondered if Joe was disappointed that he wasn't eating salmon. She watched him dip his fish into tartar sauce. He loved salmon, and oddly enough, they didn't have any on the menu at the Kodiak Grill.

"Are you sorry we didn't go into Ketchikan?" she asked with uncertainty.

"No, not at all. Why?"

"Oh, I was just thinking we should have gone to that salmon bake with Brandon. You probably would have enjoyed it better than this."

"I'd rather be right where I am."

She dropped the fry she'd been about to eat. It plopped into the ketchup. That was the last thing she expected to hear. She looked up to see if he was serious.

His gaze met hers, brown eyes steady, mouth slightly curved. She could scarcely believe it. Lisa's heart started to pound. He wanted to be here, with *her*. She'd done the right thing by coming on the cruise after all. Joe was out of the cabin, not holed up alone— brooding. Being here was a good thing. Maybe she didn't need to confess her motives after all.

A prick of her subconscious needled her. *Yes*, she did need to tell him.

"Are *you* sorry we didn't go into Ketchikan?" he asked. "If you'd like, we can go into Juneau tomorrow."

Joe, being nice to her, offering to spend time with her. A prick of guilt struck at the hope blossoming in her heart. She had to tell him. "I'm not sorry we're here, Joe. And I'd also love to go to Juneau tomorrow."

"But there is something bothering you, isn't there? I know you, Lisa, remember?"

She swallowed hard and nodded. "There's something I wanted to talk to you about."

"That's right, before my stomach interrupted."

Nerves prevented her from smiling at his attempt at humor. Her mouth felt frozen and only with God's help would she be able to get the words out.

He stood. "Would you like some more tea before we talk?"

Mutely, she nodded then watched as Joe walked away to get the tea. If things didn't go right, she'd be watching him walk away again—this time forever.

****

Great. Joe tensed as he placed the tea on the table in front of Lisa, certain she was about to ask him to come home. He *so* did not want to have this conversation. Listening to it on his answering machine everyday was one thing, sitting face-to-face with her was something else altogether.

They were both in such a mess, and he had no idea how to fix it. As much as being on this cruise had made him remember how much he wanted to be with her, he just wasn't ready. He needed to be sure he wouldn't hurt her again before he recommitted to their marriage.

Lisa sipped the tea and gave him a nervous smile.

How could he tell her he wasn't coming home? He'd be breaking her heart even further, and he would never forgive himself.

"It was the dawn, Joe." Lisa sounded nervous, her words rushed.

He looked at her, confused. Did she mean the

dawn he'd shown her early this morning? This wasn't at all what he'd expected her to say.

He relaxed a little.

"It did something to me. Ever since Cody died, I've had this emptiness inside me."

"I know. Me too." On impulse, Joe took her hand in his. He was only going to squeeze it, but her hands were cold as ice, so he didn't let go.

"I don't know if it's the same kind of emptiness, Joe. The emptiness isn't because Cody isn't here. It's different. I'm empty because…" She trailed off, closing her eyes and breathing in. When she opened them again, they were suspiciously bright.

Joe remained quiet and waited for her to go on.

"I don't know if I can explain it right now. Remember I told you this morning that I needed to spend some quiet time with God?" She pressed her lips together and shook her head. "I still do. I need to think about it some more because I don't want to make an even bigger mess of things."

"What things, Lisa?" He resisted the urge to reach for her and waited, instead, for her to continue.

She said nothing for a moment, then shook her head again. "I can't talk about it right now. I hope you understand. I—I need a little more time." She pulled her now-warm hand from his, leaving him suddenly cold.

Time for what? Unsure of what to say, Joe reached for another piece of fried fish. Lisa had just skirted something that weighed heavily on her heart. She'd share it with him when she was ready, but, oddly enough, he wanted her to share it with him now.

"Are you going to eat your pickle?"

Joe looked down at his plate and speared the

offending object with his fork then held it out to her. "I'm glad to see some things never change." The smile escaped him before he could call it back. Just as quickly, her gaze locked with his as she reached for the pickle. She smiled back, and Joe couldn't help but wonder if it was possible that things *could* get better for them.

****

After lunch, they settled back into the plush chairs on the solarium's deck. Joe seemed to lose himself in his book while Lisa couldn't concentrate on hers. She wanted to rejoice that they'd taken an important step, broken a two-month-long silence and turned a corner in their relationship. Instead, she struggled with feelings of guilt.

They couldn't have a relationship until she was honest with him, honest with God, and honest with herself.

Lisa shoved the troublesome thought away. She refused to think like that. They would always have a relationship.

After an hour or so of reading quietly, Joe stood and stretched. He looked at his watch.

"I know you haven't decided whether or not you want to go into Juneau tomorrow, but we need to decide soon. If we want to do anything in port, we have to sign up by 3:00 PM the day prior." He glanced at his watch again. "That gives us about fifteen minutes to decide."

Lisa hesitated for only a second before she nodded. They were husband and wife. They belonged together. God *wanted* them together. She'd do anything to be with Joe.

As long as I don't have to ride on the seaplane, Lord. Please?

"I think I'd like to see Juneau, so go ahead and sign us up."

"What do you want us to sign up for?" He sounded so eager that something in his tone drew on a familiar chord deep within her soul. She knew exactly what he wanted her to say.

"I don't care." Lisa tried to sound nonchalant, even though she felt anything but. "Whatever you want to do is fine with me." As soon as she spoke his gaze met hers and her heart began to hammer. She didn't want to hear his answer.

"I *want* to go on the seaplane."

The way he said it, the eagerness in his eyes, reminded her of their son. If Cody were here they'd both be begging her to fly in the plane with them. Fear pounded in her head. Did she dare push past her fright and agree to go with Joe on the little plane?

She took a deep breath. Joe was a part of Cody she could never lose. Still, to get on that plane...she didn't know if she could make herself.

"I know you don't want to, Lisa, but I think you'd enjoy it once you got over your fear."

"There's not much likelihood of that." The instant she spoke, Lisa regretted it. The disappointment on his face pricked her heart. Now she could clearly see Cody in his expression and it tugged at her heart. Refusing to do something that meant so much to Joe when she knew how badly he wanted to do it was selfish. She shouldn't let her fear get the best of her, especially when Joe had tried so hard to make her happy today. He was even planning to eat in the dining room tonight.

Would going for a ride on a seaplane show him how much she wanted to be with him and make him realize how much they needed to be together? She'd give anything if that were the case.

Even risking her life in the air.

"Go sign us up for the seaplane, Joe." Too late, the words were out and she couldn't call them back.

"Really?" His mouth curled up into a smile and ignited her heart.

Her heart picked up a beat. It was worth the risk to have him looking like this…like a man who might be starting to live again. A gentle, happy man who would be there in joy and sorrow, a man whose face would occasionally offer glimpses of the son she'd never see grow up.

Lisa nodded. "I think maybe we should offer to take Brandon and his dad." Lisa's heart pounded even as she spoke the words. "He'll love it, and we both know it's the only way he'll ever get to go."

"What about you?"

"What about me?"

"Will you be all right with this?"

"No."

The hopeful look in his eyes disappeared.

"But I'll try," she added quickly. "For Brandon. He needs something to look forward to." And so do you, she added silently. She wanted him to look forward to something. Even if that particular *something* petrified her.

"Lisa, this is great." His smile was wide now, and she wanted to revel in it.

Instead, she was so scared she couldn't answer.

"You'll love it. I know you will."

Lisa nodded and somehow managed to flash him a fake smile. But Joe never saw it because he was already halfway down the hall toward the elevator.

A terrible feeling of dread settled over her, and Lisa had a feeling she'd be awake all night trying to work up courage she wasn't sure she'd be able to find. She settled back into her lounge chair, closed her eyes, and sent a quick prayer heavenward begging to be blessed with a heaping dose of that courage.

Lisa didn't know why, but everything seemed to hinge on this seaplane ride.

13

Excited about tomorrow, Joe stepped into the elevator to head back to the Denali Deck. Just as the doors were about to shut he heard a commotion in the hall.

"Wait for us, Mr. Joe!"

He stuck a foot in between the doors to prevent them from closing.

Brandon ran toward the elevator, a harried looking Chad three steps behind. Talk about timing. Knowing he didn't have time to find Chad before signing them up for the seaplane tour, he'd gone ahead and signed them up. He'd have to find a way to distract Brandon so he could ask Chad about it.

"Where's Miss Lisa? You guys wanna eat dinner with us?"

"Brandon, stop asking so many questions."

"He's no bother, Chad." Joe tried to give Brandon a reassuring glance. "Lisa's reading a book in the solarium just down the hall from our room. You'll see her when we get off the elevator. As for dinner, thank you very much for the offer, Brandon. But we already agreed to eat with a different friend. She invited us this morning."

"Oh." Brandon kicked at the wall of the elevator.

"I'm pretty sure you'll see Lisa sometime tomorrow." Joe smiled at the boy, trying to offer him some assurance without spoiling the surprise until he spoke to Chad.

"OK." Brandon sounded disappointed.

The elevator stopped on the Denali Deck, and they stepped into the hall together. The solarium was a short distance down the hall, and Joe could see Lisa sitting in her lounge chair facing the water. It looked as though she might have fallen asleep, but he couldn't really tell from here.

"Listen, Chad, could I talk with you for a minute?"

"Sure, what's up?"

"Well..." Joe hesitated as he looked at Brandon. The boy was listening intently, as if sensing something big. "Brandon, do you mind if I talk to your dad in private? It's kind of a grownup conversation."

Chad looked at him curiously then nodded. "Brandon? Why don't you go stand over by the window for a minute?"

Brandon looked down at the floor as if trying to decide whether to obey. Finally, he shuffled off toward the window and leaned his face against it to stare out at the water.

Joe waited a second to be sure Brandon wasn't listening. When it appeared the boy was watching intently as they slowly passed a glacier, he lowered his voice. "Lisa and I have been talking. We want to thank you and Brandon for helping me find her last night. We'd like to take the both of you on a seaplane ride tomorrow."

"A seaplane?" Chad's response was louder than Joe had hoped, and Brandon was at their side in an instant.

"Can we, Dad? Can we?"

Great. Brandon had overheard. If Chad said no Brandon would be so disappointed.

Chad sighed in exasperation. Joe tensed, waiting for Chad to turn down the offer.

"Lisa and I really want to do something to show our gratitude." Joe looked at Brandon, took in his eager expression. "It would mean a lot to us if you said yes. Please?"

"Yeah, Dad. Please?"

Chad took a deep breath then let it out. "If I say yes, do you promise to behave?"

Brandon's little blond head bobbed up and down, his eager features perfectly schooled into the picture of obedience.

Joe pressed his lips together to keep his expression bland but struggled not to bust out with a smile. For such a little boy, Brandon seemed so serious. If they did go on the seaplane, the boy wouldn't be able to contain his excitement for long.

"It's awfully expensive," Chad said.

"It's worth it to us," Joe was quick to assure him.

Chad was silent for so long, Joe feared he'd say no. "OK," he finally agreed. Then he turned to Brandon. "But I won't put up with any of your wild behavior."

"Thanks, Dad!" Brandon was all smiles and looked as if he wanted to jump in the air. But he seemed to think better of it and clasped his hands in front of him as if it would help him be perfectly still. "I'll be good. I promise."

Then Brandon turned to Joe. "Thanks, Mr. Joe. Will Miss Lisa be there?"

"You're very welcome, and yes, she will." At least, he hoped she would. Even though she'd agreed, he still worried she'd change her mind.

"Oh, look," Brandon said. "There she is!" If possible, Brandon smiled even bigger as he took off running toward the solarium. A warm feeling spread through Joe's chest. The little boy was growing quite attached to Lisa.

****

It seemed she'd just nodded off when Lisa had the oddest feeling of someone standing over her. Her eyes flew open and she found herself staring into Brandon's eager face. Startled, she jumped.

"Sorry, Miss Lisa. I didn't mean to wake you up."

"Brandon. That's OK." It was kind of nice to wake up and see a little boy's smiling face, even if it wasn't *her* little boy's face. She sighed.

"What's wrong, Miss Lisa?" Brandon blue eyes clouded with concern.

She reached out and ruffled his hair. Would this painful longing for Cody ever go away? Somehow, she didn't think it would.

"Nothing for you to worry about, Brandon."

Joe was talking to Chad. She was afraid to ask the little boy if he knew about their planned seaplane adventure. "How was your day?"

"OK, I guess," Brandon answered. "The fish was kind of gross, though."

"I guess that means you'll be nice and hungry for dinner."

He nodded. "I'm nice and hungry now, though."

"We need to get you cleaned up for dinner," Chad announced.

"In a minute, Dad. I want to talk to Miss Lisa."

Chad sighed, looking like he'd spent his entire day chasing Brandon. Lisa would give anything to have spent a day like that with Cody.

"Who's Cody?"

Brandon's innocent question brought an instant lump to her throat, and for a minute she couldn't answer.

"Brandon," his dad scolded.

"It's OK." She didn't want Brandon to get in trouble for being a curious boy.

"How did you know about Cody?"

"'Cuz last night when you were crying about the whales, you said his name lots of times. Is he your boy?"

"Yes," she whispered. "He's my boy. And he wanted to see the whales for his birthday."

"How come he's not here? Did you leave him at home?"

"No." Lisa shook her head and bit into her bottom lip. She had no clue what to say.

"Brandon, that's enough. Leave the Kendalls alone."

Lisa caught Joe's eye.

"He's fine, Chad." She knelt down beside Brandon. "Brandon, honey, Cody's not at home. At least not the kind of home you and I know. My little boy is gone from us now."

Wide blue eyes gazed up at her, and her heart broke for the millionth time. "He's living with Jesus in heaven."

Brandon's mouth formed a silent *Wow!* She looked over his shoulder to see Chad's reaction, knowing full well some adults didn't want the words Jesus, God, or heaven spoken to their children. Chad, however, didn't seem to mind. Instead, he appeared to be listening with interest.

"How'd he get there?"

As most of his previous questions had, this one brought a twinge of pain. Brandon was certainly inquisitive. But she wanted to answer. His innocence and sincerity stole her heart. She swallowed hard.

"There was an accident. A car accident." She blinked hard to clear her vision. But it blurred again when his warm little-boy hand tucked its way into hers.

"I bet he's happy there. My mom talked about Jesus a lot. I bet your boy and Jesus are having lots of fun."

Unable to speak, Lisa could only nod.

"Is that why you're sad? 'Cuz you don't got your boy?"

Tears stung the back of her eyes. "That's right. I'll always be a little sad."

"Just the way I'm always sad that I don't got my mom no more." He looked up at her with those wide blue eyes, and Lisa fought to control her tears. Off in the distance, she heard Chad clear his throat. That explained why the two of them were on a cruise ship alone. It also explained why Brandon had attached himself to Lisa.

She knelt down. "Come here, honey." She pulled Brandon close and held him tight, reveling that her arms were filled with the warmth and goodness of once again holding a sweaty little boy.

Brandon hugged her back for a minute before he squirmed to get away.

"We both needed that," she whispered in his ear before letting him go.

"Maybe my mom knows him," Brandon said quietly. "Cody, I mean. Maybe she'll even make a birthday cake for him. They might be friends in heaven."

"I'll bet they are, sweetie. In fact, I'm positive of it. You and I are friends now, so it only makes sense that they would be friends, too."

Brandon scrubbed the back of his hands across his eyes. Then he looked away as if embarrassed to be caught with tears in his eyes.

Lisa stood as Brandon ran over to his father. Chad stood with Joe, and both men looked uncomfortable. Chad was tucking a handkerchief into his pocket. "Sorry about that." Chad avoided her gaze and patted Brandon on the top of his head. "We need to go get ready for dinner."

Lisa nodded and waved at Brandon. He appeared so upset she offered him a smile of reassurance.

While father and son walked toward the elevator, she forced her smile to stay in place as long as possible. Brandon was almost out of sight when the smile gave way to tears. She turned her back so Joe wouldn't see, not wanting him to feel uncomfortable and see her as weak and needy. He must have sensed her need though. In a breath, his hand touched her shoulder. A second later he turned her to face him and drew her into his arms.

****

As they headed back to the cabin to dress for dinner, Lisa tried to muster some excitement. But her encounter with Brandon left her emotionally worn out. Joe went into the bathroom to get ready for dinner first, and Lisa sat on the bottom bunk to wait for him. She worried he might change his mind about dinner.

They had broken fragile ground today, and she couldn't help but worry that he might regret the things they'd talked about.

She didn't realize she'd fallen asleep until Joe gently shook her and told her it was her turn to get ready. She blinked and scrubbed her hand across her eyes. She couldn't really be awake.

Clean shaven with his still damp hair freshly combed, Joe looked like he'd stepped out of one of her dreams. One where she dreamed that nothing in their life had changed. He looked more relaxed than she'd seen him in months, and he had a gentle smile on his face. Proof he looked forward to their dinner together.

"Lisa?"

She couldn't seem to take her eyes off the dab of shaving cream he'd missed. Just a smear. High up on his cheekbone. Should she dab it off?

Wow. Twelve dozen nerves descended on her, making her mouth freeze and the words stick in her throat. Her knees almost knocked together. She'd better leave well enough alone. He would probably misinterpret the action and run scared, and she didn't want to push her luck.

"Lisa?" Joe repeated himself and as she stared at him, his smile disappeared. "I don't know if these are good enough for the dining room."

Lisa realized he thought she was judging his clothing.

"No, Joe. You look great. I don't think you have to be dressed in a tux to eat there. Jessica told me it was nice, but not formal. I'm sure she wouldn't tell me that if it wasn't true."

"I don't even have a suit jacket with me."

"I'm sure it's fine. If not, we'll just leave." She offered him a wide smile, trying to reassure him. It wasn't hard to smile, given she would be dining with her husband.

"You'd better get ready." He gestured toward the door.

"Oh, yeah." She tore her gaze from his face and headed to the closet to grab her dress. What would Joe think when he saw her in it? Would his reaction be anything like hers had just been?

Please, Lord, let it bring back good memories for him.

****

What was taking her so long?

Looking at his watch for the sixth time in as many minutes, Joe tapped his foot impatiently. It had been over fifteen minutes since Lisa went into the bathroom to dress for dinner. Not that he was in any big hurry to go eat in a dining room with a bunch of strangers. He just didn't like waiting.

"Joe?" Her voice was soft, almost timid. When he turned from the window, he knew why.

Wow.

Her dress, a tiny little thing in a dark blue velvety fabric, hugged her in all the right places and highlighted the blue of her eyes. It reminded him of one of the happiest times in his life. Their wedding night when Lisa had first worn that dress.

Once again the thought ran through his mind that she'd come here in order to try to talk him into going home. He quickly dismissed it. She really hadn't been doing anything to push him in that direction. So then why was she wearing this particular dress tonight? More curiously, why had she even brought it along?

"Lisa." Great. He sounded breathless, like an awkward teenager on his first date. Hopefully she hadn't noticed. "You look gorgeous."

A shy look washed over her features as Joe stood staring like an idiot. For a split second, he wanted to turn and run. But he couldn't do that to her. He'd already hurt her enough. In ways he could never atone for.

Trapped, he smoothed the front of his shirt. "Are you...um, sure this is OK for the dining room?"

Lisa laughed. "I already told you, you look perfect. Anyway, isn't it the woman who is supposed to ask those questions? Next you'll be asking me if you look fat." She laughed again.

It had been far too long since Joe heard that sound, and he loved it. He could listen to it forever. He hoped he'd be able to hear it again at dinner in a romantic setting—after all this time. Especially with Lisa wearing that dress?

The nerves started dancing in his stomach again.

"Well." Joe reached for the doorknob, and they stared at each other awkwardly. "Let's go."

Unable to help himself, he put his hand on Lisa's back as they headed toward the elevator. Warmth suffused him, and he blamed it on the dress. It drew him directly into dangerous territory.

Once they stepped into the elevator, he made sure to keep a good three feet between them.

Even three feet away was too close. She smelled too good. She smiled nervously but didn't say anything.

Following Jessica's directions, they found the Aurora Borealis dining room on the Tlingit Deck without any trouble. Lisa turned to Joe. "See, I told you it would be fine."

Looking around, Joe relaxed a little. Plenty of men

were dressed just like he was.

"What about me? Does this dress make me look fat?" She laughed again and her blue eyes sparkled. For a quick second the years seemed to melt away. It was almost as if they were dating again—young lovers, happy, their entire lives ahead of them. He longed to kiss her. He searched her face before he reached out and brushed her cheek. Her lips parted and her eyes grew wide.

"Your hair." He knew he sounded lame, and he made a show of smoothing the curls that caressed her cheek. "We must have encountered some wind between here and our cabin." He knew full well that hadn't happened.

"Um, yeah." She nodded, but the hopeful glimmer in her eyes said that she'd seen right through him. He was deeply drawn to her tonight. Not that a day ever went by when he didn't think of her, long for her, and wish for a chance to turn back the clock and change things. But tonight was different...and impossible.

He'd do his best to remember and accept that. He didn't deserve a second chance. Moreover, Lisa deserved not to be burdened by his brokenness.

"Joe, Lisa, over here."

Snapped from his wistfulness, Joe followed Lisa to Jessica's table. Surprisingly, Chad and Brandon were there as well.

"Hi, Miss Lisa." Brandon's face lit up.

"Hi, Brandon." Lisa smiled at the boy, her smile so bright and genuine it rushed from Joe's head to his heart then to his toes. No wonder the little boy was enamored of her.

The large table was round, and there was a space for two between Jessica and Brandon. Chad sat on the other side of his son. On the opposite side of the table, between Chad and Jessica, sat a guy in his mid-thirties. He nodded a greeting and gave Lisa the once-over. Joe clenched his jaw as he returned the nod.

"Here, Lisa." Joe pulled out the chair next to Brandon, knowing she'd want to sit by the little boy. He was rewarded with a wide smile, and before he realized what he'd done, he winked at her.

Again, he caught a whiff of whatever she'd showered with. He inhaled and found himself scooting his chair closer to her as he sat.

While Lisa, Jessica, and Brandon exchanged pleasantries, Chad sat in silence and the man across the table looked on expectantly.

In Joe's estimation, the man could only be described as suave and debonair. But his demeanor was so obviously fake. Joe didn't like the interested look in the other man's eye, so he deliberately said nothing.

Apparently uncomfortable, Lisa finally extended her hand across the table. "Hi, I'm Lisa." Then she speared Joe with a pointed look of chastisement.

He raised one shoulder halfway. Why should he have to introduce her to a shark with a predatory gleam in his eye?

"I'm Darryl. Pleased to meet you." Darryl held Lisa's hand a little too long.

"I'm Lisa's husband, Joe." In one swift motion, Joe grabbed Lisa's right hand from Darryl's and tucked it in his own left hand.

Lisa looked at him in shock, as did Jessica. He was surprised himself, but not displeased. Lisa's hand was where it should be—clasped in his, not some smarmy stranger's.

14

After the waiter finished pouring water for Lisa and Joe, everyone placed their order. Joe eyed Darryl to make sure he focused his attention somewhere other than on Lisa. Chad fussed with Brandon over something. Lisa and Jessica chatted about Jessica's day in Ketchikan.

"Miss Jessica, Miss Jessica!" Brandon tugged on Jessica's sleeve, eager to get her attention. When she and Lisa stopped talking, he burst in to the conversation. "I get to go on a seaplane tomorrow. Miss Lisa and Mr. Joe are coming, too."

"Are they?"

Joe detected a hint of interest in Jessica's response.

"Hey!" Brandon's face lit up. "Why don't you come with us?"

"That would be kind of fun, Brandon." Jessica beamed and nodded. "A real adventure. I need more adventure in my life."

Joe smiled. After living all these years on a farm in a small town in Washington, Jessica decided she needed adventure. While he pondered that, he became aware of the music playing in the background just as it changed to a melody he and Lisa always considered "theirs." A fierce wave of longing struck him, and he could barely swallow. They'd played the tune at their wedding, and they'd danced to it on their honeymoon at dinner.

The song, the dress Lisa wore, the tulips she'd bought yesterday and put in the cabin…Again, he had to wonder if Lisa had set up this whole thing, if she'd tricked him into rehashing memories.

No. Joe shook the thought from his mind. He'd been with Lisa since long before they entered the dining room, and she'd never left the table. Besides, Jessica was the one who'd invited them to dinner. And Lisa surely hadn't planned what happened yesterday with the whales and her despair over missing them. It was a coincidence. Nothing more. Lisa didn't have a deceitful bone in her body.

Just as the singer asked if they could share a life's worth of dances, a deep voice startled Joe out of his thoughts.

"Excuse me. Would you care to dance?"

Joe looked up to see Darryl bending over Lisa's hand. It looked like he was preparing to kiss it. The urge to plant his fist in the guy's face was strong—overwhelming.

It didn't escape his notice that Jessica looked on with interest.

Lisa gently pulled her hand from Darryl's, glancing over at Joe at the same time. Much as he wanted to deck Darryl, he didn't want to come across as jealous. Especially after he'd grabbed her hand from Darryl's earlier, and certainly not after he'd been pushing her away for months. "It's fine, Lisa." He nodded slowly, heartsick. "Go ahead and dance with him."

Lisa's eyes widened and he thought he detected a look of disgust as she turned from him to gaze up at Darryl. Joe's heart seemed to freeze in mid-beat, and he held his breath while he waited for Lisa to answer

Darryl.

"I'm sorry." She politely declined, and Joe's heart started to beat again. "Thank you, though."

There was no hint of disgust in her voice, which told Joe the look had been meant solely for him.

Silence reigned at the table as Darryl walked away. *Most likely to find some other guy's wife to dance with.* Though Joe's thoughts were cynical, the relief that coursed through him was unmistakable.

Jessica studied them both intently, her gaze never wavering. Though it hadn't taken long for Joe to feel a fondness for her, right now he wished she'd disappear. It didn't make matters easier when Chad and Brandon stared at him. He wished they'd disappear as well. Did everyone here know their business? It became clear they were neither leaving nor looking away from what he wanted to be a private moment.

He very much wanted to talk to Lisa alone.

Darryl chose that moment to return and take his place at the table.

"If you'll excuse me, I'm going to powder my nose."

Darryl and Chad both half-rose from their chairs the instant Lisa stood. Before Joe could stand himself, she was gone.

"Don't worry, Joe." Jessica reached over and squeezed his hand. "Things will be fine." Jessica spoke in a reassuring voice, her tone low so the others wouldn't hear.

"No, Jessica. They won't. My son is gone. Lisa's heart is breaking all over again. Nothing will ever be fine again."

Joe pulled his hand from Jessica's and pressed his lips together. His marriage was in shambles. Lisa's heart was broken. His heart ached all the time. They each carried around a burden of guilt neither one of them knew how to erase. He was so sick of people saying everything would be OK. He'd heard it so many times in the past several months he hoped never to hear it again.

Still, as he watched Jessica's expression change from encouragement to distress, he realized he'd upset her. She'd meant well, as did everyone else who offered him words of hope. "I'm sorry, Jessica. I didn't mean to raise my voice. I'm just so...I don't know...tired, I guess. Tired of waiting to get over it." A dull ache filled his heart and he avoided Jessica's eye.

"You're right, Joe. That isn't what I meant. You will never forget that boy, and you'll always hurt over losing him. But your life won't be this hopeless and dark forever."

"I tried, Jessica, but it didn't work very well."

"What do you mean?"

"Lisa refused to go to Ketchikan this morning."

"Yes, but she ate breakfast with you on the balcony. And she's here with you tonight. Didn't she agree to go to Juneau tomorrow? I think you're doing just fine."

"Yeah, but she's in the bathroom crying right now." It didn't escape his notice that Brandon, Chad, and even Darryl—the last person he wanted to know his business—stared intently.

"That isn't your fault."

"Yes, it is."

Jessica opened her mouth to protest then seemed to think better of it. She took a sip of water and looked him square in the eye. "OK, maybe it is. You shouldn't have—" She cast a glance around the table. Chad and

Darryl both picked up their water glasses and avoided her gaze. Jessica lowered her voice to a whisper. "You shouldn't have told Lisa it was all right for her to dance with a strange man."

"You're right, I shouldn't have. I'm not even sure why I did it. I don't know what to do anymore. All I know is I've upset her even more."

Jessica sighed and rose from the table. "Come on, Joe. Let's go for a little walk." She waited while Joe stood, then she took hold of his elbow.

Before he followed her out of the dining room, Joe turned and said good night to Brandon and Chad. And much as he still didn't want to, to Darryl.

Once they were well away from the dining room, Jessica steered them to an empty bench along the passageway.

"Look," she said once they were seated. "Lisa is going to cry now and again. Maybe even for the rest of her life. You are, too. If you'd let yourself *feel*."

Joe looked away, not wanting Jessica to know how much he tried *not* to feel.

"You know, whether you want to admit it or not, you're trying to help Lisa. And she's trying to help you. But neither of you can see that by helping each other, you're also helping yourselves."

"Helping myself, how?" That made no sense.

"You've put yourself out on a limb to help Lisa. You'd rather hide yourself away from the world. But you see Lisa's need, so you're trying to make her feel better. You can't sit there and tell me you don't feel better, too."

"I don't," he said quickly.

Jessica peered at him over her glasses. "Not in the least? Be honest with yourself even if you won't be honest with me."

OK, he admitted to himself. Maybe he did feel a little better. Jessica must have seen something on his face, because a slow smile spread across hers.

"See? It's the Lord. He's calling you. You may not even be aware of it, but He's seeking you. By helping Lisa, you're digging yourself out of that deep dark place and seeing a little bit of light. The same thing is happening to her. You mark my words, Joe. By the end of this cruise, neither of you will be the same again."

He wanted it to be true. He didn't deserve it, but he wanted it nonetheless.

****

Lisa approached the table at the same moment the waiter arrived with their food. It was a good thing, because she needed a diversion. She'd left the table to get her hurt and frustration under control, but it still threatened to bubble over. Joe had pretty clearly broadcast his eagerness for her to dance with a strange man.

Everything seemed fine until that song had played through the speakers of the dining room. It seemed meant to be. Perfect timing. God's timing. Only He knew what that song meant to them.

It would have been the perfect moment for them if Darryl hadn't interrupted. He'd spoiled everything. But the look on Joe's face when he said he didn't care if she danced with Darryl—like he wished the guy would take her off of his hands—hurt her deeply and spoiled it even more. Joe's actions totally contradicted the spark she'd seen in his eyes when they'd first walked into the dining room and he'd brushed the hair from her face. That spark was the only thing she could grab on to for hope that he was coming around to her way of thinking.

"I don't see any powder on your nose, Miss Lisa."

Laughter spilled around the table at Brandon's innocent comment. One look into the little boy's questioning gaze, and Lisa's heart melted.

"It's not the kind you can see, sweetheart."

"Oh." He appeared to give it some serious thought. Unable to help herself, Lisa smiled at him. At the same time, her anger at Joe dispersed. Smiling at Brandon while she felt angry toward Joe or anyone else at the same time was next to impossible.

Before she could take her seat, Joe and Jessica approached from behind. She hadn't even noticed they weren't at the table.

Joe held Jessica's chair for her as she sat down, then he turned to Lisa.

"Come with me, Lisa." He grabbed her by the hand before she could even protest.

And Jessica had a smile—no, a smirk—on her face.

"Where are we going?" His hand felt so right in hers that she didn't even think of pulling away, even if she was still a little miffed at him.

"I just want to talk to you for a minute."

Immediately curious, Lisa allowed Joe to lead her away from the table.

As he did, she heard Brandon ask loudly, "Where are they going, Dad?"

Certain the question attracted stares from every nearby table, Lisa hurried alongside Joe. She didn't care what people thought. She only cared that her husband wanted to talk to her, though she was curious about why he led her in the direction of the dance floor instead of the entrance to the dining room.

"Is there a reason we can't talk at the table?" Even as she asked the question, her heart picked up a beat. She thought she'd detected a look of relief on his face when she refused to dance with Darryl. Had Darryl caused Joe to realize he was ready to come home? Oh, if he would only tell her so. Her heart quickened.

"Too many people are listening."

"You mean Jessica?"

"And Chad and Brandon and Derrick."

"Darryl."

"Whatever."

He lowered his voice, and Lisa noticed an immediate softening to his tone. "Let's dance."

Her heart picked up another beat, thrumming in her ears. "You're willing to dance with me rather than talk in front of them?" She tried to suppress a smile. Joe's mysterious act certainly gave her reason to hope. He grabbed her hand before she could question him or refuse. Not that she *would* refuse, of course.

With her hand clasped tightly in his, Lisa rested her head against his broad shoulder. There was nowhere else on earth she belonged. Listening to the beating of his heart, she didn't even try to suppress her sigh. This was so perfect.

The familiar scent of soap and shaving cream almost brought tears to her eyes. It had been so long. She tried to inhale without him knowing. She closed her eyes as she did, savoring the familiar scent. Could she possibly draw enough of it into her senses to last her a lifetime in case the unthinkable happened and he didn't come home?

"We'll just be a minute. We need to talk." His warm breath brushed across her ear as he whispered the words, but it took a moment for them to register. When they finally did, the cloud of perfection vanished.

Need, not *want*. This didn't sound as promising as she'd first thought. Joe didn't sound like he wanted to dance *or* talk. "About?" Again, her heart picked up a beat. But not in a good way. She was afraid to look up at him, afraid for him to see her desperation.

Joe swallowed hard, and she could feel him hesitate before he spoke again. "Why didn't you dance with him?"

Her response was simple. "We're married, Joe."

"I know that but—"

"But nothing. You're my husband, and there's nothing, *nothing* you can do to change it."

Before he could respond, she continued. "Today was a wonderful day. It was all so perfect. You made me feel better at a time when I didn't think I'd ever feel better again. You may not think you need me, but I sure need you. You're the only man for me, Joe. I'm the only woman for you. When are you going to quit torturing both of us and let us come back to each other?"

Pushing away from his arms, she stared up at him. The pain etched on his face and in his eyes was so gripping, Lisa couldn't look away.

"I want to dance with you, Joe. *Only* you. And, like the song they were playing earlier says, *our* song in case you need a reminder, for the rest of my life."

"Oh, so you noticed it, too?"

"What?" She wasn't questioning his words. She simply couldn't believe he'd noticed the tune when it was playing.

"Never mind." He glanced away, sounding like he

wished he'd kept quiet.

"Joe?" She didn't know why, but she wanted him to admit he'd heard the song, wanted him to make eye contact so she could see what it meant to him.

And it did mean something to him. She could tell by the way that he still refused to look at her.

She kept her gaze steady, staring at his profile, wanting him to know how serious she was about saving their marriage. Even when her eyes filled with the tears she so desperately fought, tears she didn't want Joe to see, she didn't waver.

Lisa wanted Joe to look her in the eyes and tell her he was coming home.

Either that or give her a good reason why not.

Susan Diane Johnson

15

Holding Lisa close was Joe's second mistake. The first was the bright idea to dance with her.

Every ounce of self-preservation was lost when he asked the question that propelled them to the dance floor in the first place.

What on earth was he thinking?

Simply put, he wasn't. Not in the least. Not about getting off this ship without losing his heart all over again, that's for sure. He'd stopped processing gray matter the instant he stared into her bright blue eyes, still swimming with tears, and he was lost along with every ounce of self-preservation.

Small, slender, and soft, her hand fit perfectly in his, and as they walked to the dance floor he was slammed with memories. Her hand trembled slightly. Clearly, it affected her as well as it did him. He shouldn't be doing this to her. It wasn't fair.

Mistake number three came when they reached the dance floor where couples had their arms wrapped around each other. Either Joe took Lisa in his arms, or he'd look like a fool.

Knowing how she affected him, he'd almost rather look the fool. But he'd come this far, he would finish it.

As soon as he put her arms around her waist, he was a goner.

Heaven help him. How could he stay away from her?

Tenderness pulled Joe's heart toward Lisa. After all of the guilt he'd heaped upon himself, after all of the time away from her, it simply didn't make sense. Was it the setting? The music? Or when he'd brushed the hair from her cheek when they'd first arrived in the dining room? Or...simply Lisa.

Now, as she stared him down expecting some kind of an answer, something stirred inside him—a new admiration. Who was this new Lisa who didn't look away at the slightest bit of eye contact? This new side of her, this quiet strength, and the way he responded to it, unnerved him.

Even though he stood his ground in avoiding her gaze, she continued to stare at him. Expectant. Determined.

Thankfully, the music ended, giving him the perfect opportunity to turn and head back to the table. Though he tried not to be, he was well aware of her hand in his as she ran along behind him.

Knowing full well he was acting rude, Joe didn't slow his stride. Neither did he hold the chair for her when they reached the table.

When he caught sight of Jessica's disapproving glare, he withered. Shame filled him. This dinner tonight was about Lisa, not him or his petty jealousy or even about the feelings he tried not to have.

He turned to Lisa and the hurt in her eyes pricked his conscience. Yet, again, he had to swallow his pride. "I'm sorry. I was in a hurry to get back to the table so we could eat."

He could tell she didn't believe him. Neither did Jessica, but at least she stopped glaring at him long enough to pick at her food.

No one said grace. It was an odd thing to notice,

but Joe was thinking about God again. Saying grace was something they'd always done before he started paying more attention to his job and less to his family. There were many nights when Lisa and Cody ate by themselves. Had they said grace as they sat in the quiet house alone? If only he could get back every one of those missed meals.

Lisa hadn't said grace when they'd eaten together earlier. Or maybe she had, and he hadn't noticed. Falling back into a relationship with the Lord seemed more natural by the minute, and he figured he'd start to notice a lot of things.

Joe bowed his head briefly, asking God to forgive him and to take away Lisa's pain. As for his own pain, he didn't deserve to have it taken away.

He froze for a moment while he realized he could do one of two things. Embrace the renewing of the relationship or run. He blinked his eyes, feeling God's presence all around him. He wasn't sure how this would affect his relationship with Lisa, but he could no longer run from God.

As he finished his prayer, he avoided eye contact with everyone—especially Lisa—and reached for the steak sauce.

****

Lisa's heart filled with joy when Joe bowed his head to pray. In all honesty, she couldn't remember the last time she saw him pray before a meal. Her thoughts were interrupted by a squeal from Brandon.

"What's wrong?" Chad's sharp tone was followed by a loud sigh, and caught Lisa off guard. It must have done the same for everyone else, too, because they all stared at Chad.

A deep red flush that contrasted sharply with the shade of his hair crept across Chad's face. "Sorry," he said. "What's wrong, Brandon?" This time the question was asked in a softer tone.

"There's something icky on my sandwich." Brandon pushed his plate away and wrinkled his nose.

How many times had she seen that same look on Cody's face? Lisa smiled in spite of herself, amazed when the memory brought a smile instead of pain. She caught Joe's eye, and she saw a faint hint of a smile on his face as well. It disappeared so fast though, she might have only imagined it.

"Brandon." Chad groaned with obvious frustration. "It's a turkey sandwich. Turkey and mayo. Maybe a little lettuce."

"No, Dad. This man-aze is gross. It's all lumpy. And there's something else in here. Some pink thing that I don't like."

Chad sighed again and reached for Brandon's plate. "Let me see." He pulled the top slice of bread off to reveal what appeared to be cream cheese with some sort of cranberry mixture. Lisa had to agree with Brandon. It did look gross.

Chad grabbed a butter knife and started scraping the bread. "Really, Brandon." Chad's tone was stern now instead of frustrated. "We can't afford to waste food. You need to learn to eat things you don't like."

Tears hovered in Brandon's eyes. "But, Dad—"

"No buts. Just eat."

Empathy for Brandon welled deep within.

"Chad?" Jessica sounded nervous, almost as if she wasn't sure saying anything was a good idea. "Brandon's welcome to have my mashed potatoes and gravy. There's even a dinner roll here he might like."

"And he can have some of my steak," Joe offered. His voice was deeper than usual and carefully controlled.

"No, thank you. That's nice of you, but Brandon needs to learn to eat things he doesn't like."

Brandon looked truly distressed, and the discomfort of everyone at their table was palpable.

"But, Dad, there's still stuff stuck to the bread. I might puke."

"No," Chad growled. "You. Won't. Now. Eat."

Lisa didn't hear what, if anything, Brandon said because Joe chose that moment to shove his chair back and storm from the dining room. He didn't even excuse himself.

"Joe!" Lisa stood as she called out to him, but he didn't respond or look back.

"It'll be all right, dear." Jessica patted Lisa's hand and gave her a tiny smile.

No, it wouldn't. Lisa sat back down and tried returning the smile, but it was weak at best. When she heard Brandon ask if Joe was angry at someone, she grabbed her napkin and blotted her eyes in hopes of stopping the tears that threatened to spill down her cheeks.

"Give him a few minutes, dear, and then go after him."

Lisa looked Jessica square in the eye and spoke with as much confidence as she could muster. "Oh, I will, Jessica. I will."

He's upset. He's hurting and he needs me.

Her unspoken words bolstered her to her feet.

She stood and walked from the dining room, determined to find her husband.

Joe wasn't outside the dining room as she expected. She hurried to their cabin, hoping he went back there. The cabin was empty, but Lisa could smell Joe's aftershave in the air.

She could sit here and wait for him to return, but he'd looked for her last night when she needed him. She intended to return the favor.

Lisa left the cabin, got in the elevator, and pushed the button for the Skygazer Deck. That's where Joe found her last night, and that's where she hoped to find him now.

To Lisa's relief, he stood against the railing across from the Skygazer Café.

He stared out at the inky black water, the look on his face forlorn. The look tugged at her, and she longed to wrap her arms around his waist and press her face against his shoulders—broad shoulders carrying an even broader burden. But something in her whispered, *be still*. So she was. Though the ache to hold him was strong, she sat at one of the nearby outdoor tables and remained silent.

Eventually Joe buried his face in something he held in his hands. She hadn't noticed it before, and from this distance, she couldn't quite tell what it was.

After a few minutes that seemed to last forever, he walked over and sat next to Lisa even though he'd never once given a hint that he knew she was there.

She gasped as he spread something on the table and smoothed it out. She realized it was her whale sweatshirt. Not Cody's, but hers.

"I wish I'd—" His words were thick with emotion.

"Wish you'd what?"

"It's too late to—" He shook his head as his voice trailed off.

"Joe?" He wasn't making any sense, and she so desperately wanted to help him.

"It doesn't matter anymore." He looked at her, studying her face. The emotion in his eyes broke her heart. She knew then she'd failed. "You shouldn't have come, Lisa."

"I wanted to make sure you were OK."

"I didn't mean just now. I meant—" He sighed. "I meant you shouldn't have come on the cruise. I knew it was a mistake when I didn't get off the ship in Vancouver."

Lisa bit her lip and shook her head. The progress they'd made—it was all coming undone. She reached out and ran her hand over the shirt, over Cody's artwork.

"It hurts too much." Joe's voice was thick with pain, but he placed his hand next to hers and traced the whale on the shirt. "Seeing you, seeing this, feeling again. I don't want to *feel*, Lisa."

"I know." She put her hand on his, oddly comforted when he made no move to escape her touch.

"And Chad...the way he treated Brandon." He looked at her and her heart twisted in anguish at the raw pain in his eyes. "He humiliated that little boy. A turkey sandwich spread with cranberries and cream cheese is not important in the scheme of things. What's important is that he has his son." Joe turned his hand up so their palms touched.

"How can he treat his son like that while mine is lying in a cold grave?"

Naked emotion tore from him, and Lisa was shocked when a tear he fought hard to suppress rolled down his face. Unable to help herself, Lisa pulled her hand from his and threw her arms around him. She cradled his head against her shoulder, blessedly thankful when he didn't resist. Instead, he buried it there while he sobbed. Tears ran freely down Lisa's face as well, but she was careful not to even sniffle. She needed to comfort Joe. This was the first time he'd sought it, and to her knowledge these were the first tears he'd shed since their son's death.

After a while, Joe grew quiet. His sobs subsided with the exception of an occasional sniffle and a deep intake of breath.

Still, he kept his head on Lisa's shoulder, and she was glad to hold him.

"Earlier, when I told you seeing Cody's artwork yesterday helped me to picture his face again...there was more. I'm not really sure why, but I need to share it with you now."

As soon as he mentioned Cody, Lisa held her breath, thankful Joe was opening up to her, eager to hear whatever it was he had to say.

"I prayed. And when I did, something inside me changed."

Hope bloomed in her heart. *Thank you, Father, for answering my prayer.*

Joe was turning back to the Lord. She'd noticed him bowing his head at dinner, before eating, but she'd thought he could have been thinking about something else. Unable to help herself, she tightened her arms around him. Joe lifted his head and studied her face for a moment. Then Lisa remained breathless when he brought his hand to her cheek and gently traced it.

"Lisa," he whispered raggedly. His eyes still held traces of tears and emotion as he tilted his face to hers and lightly caressed her lips with his own. The welcome, familiar warmth of his lips against hers left her weak in the knees, and she leaned into him.

Her heart swelled with love for this man who was so hurt he'd isolated himself from her for so long. This man—her husband. She longed to pull his head closer, to entwine her fingers through his hair, to deepen the kiss. But she held back, uncertain.

As much as her heart soared from the gentle touch of his lips on hers, she didn't know if it was a kiss of gratitude or a kiss from a man who wanted to rekindle a relationship with his wife. What did it mean?

Pondering these things, hesitant, Lisa was surprised to feel the warmth of Joe's hand claiming hers. Elated, she let him lead her back to their cabin, her pulse pounding, hope soaring.

****

Joe fumbled for the key card with one hand while holding Lisa tight with his other. She belonged in his arms, at his side. This was home. This was where he belonged. Not just for tonight, for a brief moment, but forever. He pushed the door open and reached in for the light, reluctant to let go of her even for a moment.

Shyly, Lisa looked up at him. "Joe, shall I put on some music?" A wash of bright pink color spread across her cheeks.

"OK." He let go of her briefly while she pulled out her cell phone and accessed the music application. The music wasn't in stereo, but the tune and the vocalist were clear enough.

An old song, but *their* song nonetheless.

He held his arms open and breathed in slowly, deeply, when she stepped into them. She belonged in his arms. He breathed in the scent of her soap and shampoo, and it assailed his senses. It was as if he'd stepped into a place that could only be found in his dreams...a place he didn't deserve to be. Holding her was like a balm to his battered heart. If only he could forget for five minutes that he didn't deserve to hold her, to savor her.

The rhythm of the music, the warmth of her body pressed against his, the gentle motion of the boat—it was easy to get lost in all of it.

Joe rested his cheek against the top of Lisa's head, his arms wrapped around her shoulders, hers around his waist.

It took him back to happier times, the happiest of his life—their wedding night.

What had happened to those two innocent youths with nothing ahead of them but love?

Lisa sighed and snuggled closer. Savoring the moment, Joe was caught off guard when she tilted her head up to rub her cheek against his.

Before he even realized it, he was kissing her. Time fell away, and they really were two innocent people on their honeymoon, with their lives ahead of them. How easy it would be to give in to the feeling, to forget. Maybe then he could forgive himself. But he couldn't. He didn't deserve to forget, and he certainly didn't deserve forgiveness.

Abruptly he stepped back, frightened to realize how close he really had come to forgetting Cody. He couldn't afford to lower his guard again.

One look at the pain slicing through Lisa's eyes and across her face, and his defensive guard was back. Joe looked toward the door, wanting to dash through it.

"It's OK, Joe. I understand. You can go now."

For a split second, Joe actually considered it. But he didn't have the energy to sit in a lounge or bar and listen to the noise or make small talk with strangers. And it was way too chilly to sit out on one of the outside decks.

Feeling like a fool, he sank into the chair nearest the bunk beds and closed his eyes. Opening them again, he let his gaze rest on Lisa, and he sighed. "We can't do that again, Lisa. I can't—" He broke off. There were so many words in his heart, words of love and words of doubt. He wasn't sure which ones were the right ones to say. Some would hurt her, and some might give her hope for their relationship. He didn't want to do either.

Resting his elbows on his knees, Joe buried his face in his hands. He needed to think. He really had to get a hold of himself before it was too late. If he wasn't careful, he'd be back with Lisa, and Cody's memory would fade away as they made new memories. He couldn't let that happen. He didn't deserve to be happy any more than his son deserved to be dead.

If only he could turn back the clock—redo the last few years, be a better father, a better husband—would Cody be here with them now? If only. He would give anything if he could make that happen. But he couldn't. One thing Joe had learned: life was so unfair.

He would never again have the chance to be a better father.

But he did have the chance to be a better husband. Lisa would welcome him with open arms. But if he did go back home with her how long would it be before he started working late, putting his work ahead of her, and neglecting her? Wanting to change wasn't enough, and he was too emotionally beat to put out the effort.

****

Joe wasn't sure how long he sat on the chair thinking about things, but when he got up to stretch his muscles, he discovered he was alone. He'd been so self-absorbed that Lisa had slipped out without him even noticing.

She was trying to give him space. She was thoughtful that way. It was one of the things he loved about her, her innate sense of what others needed. Even if it meant sitting outside in the cold. The realization propelled him toward the door. Lisa wouldn't set foot in a lounge or a bar. Not even if the alternative was to freeze.

Joe hoped she'd brought her jacket this time. He wasn't up for a repeat of last night, and she wasn't either. Just in case, he went back and grabbed her sweatshirt from the back of the chair where she'd dropped it when they'd returned earlier.

He went straight to the Skygazer Deck. Lisa wouldn't have gone anywhere else.

Other than Lisa, the deck was deserted. But rather than sit in one of the lounge chairs, she sat on the cold deck itself, close to the railing.

Twilight with the glaciers in the background was a sight to behold. But Joe only had eyes for Lisa as she sat there looking alone, lost, and vulnerable. He could see the naked pain on her face as she continued to stare out at the water.

Joe knew Lisa almost as well as he knew himself, and he was willing to bet she didn't see any of the breathtaking scenery. She was dwelling on him, them, and what had almost happened. What *she* wanted to happen.

She was trying to save their marriage. He knew her belief system, what she thought and felt. He wasn't misreading her signals. But it couldn't happen. As much as he loved her, as much as he wanted them to be together forever, he now understood they could never go back. He would always be broken. He had to get out of her life so she could start over.

As he stepped closer, Lisa shivered. Guilt sliced through him, and he was at her side in an instant. He touched her shoulder; her skin was like ice. He tugged the sweatshirt down over her head and helped her slip her arms into the sleeves. Then he helped her to her feet and pulled her close. She went into his arms willingly, and he didn't think about anything but Lisa and helping her get warm.

In silence, she let him lead her to their cabin, and as they walked through the door, he was relieved that her teeth were no longer chattering.

He sat her on the bed and pulled off her shoes. After removing his, he sat next to her. Pulling her close, he lay back against the pillows and wrapped the blankets around them. She started to relax as the warmth took hold, and soon she was asleep. He pressed a kiss to her head, letting his lips linger a moment too long. Holding her in his arms was so right, so perfect. He closed his eyes, savoring the feel of her.

He'd hold her close tonight and memorize every detail of her so he could remember it forever.

16

Lisa awoke in a cocoon of warmth and love. Wrapped in Joe's arms, her head on his chest, she listened to the rhythmic beat of his heart. She sighed, feeling content, and let her eyes drift shut.

She'd spent the night in Joe's arms—someplace she'd feared she'd never be again.

Something happened last night. Something big that signified a change in Joe. He was turning back to the Lord, and he'd eventually come home to her. That she was here in his arms proved it. He may not be willing to accept it now, but he wouldn't be able to deny forever that he loved her.

Missing the whales had been a low point for Lisa, but Joe's seeking her out and bringing her back to the room...his taking care of her that night, then spending the entire next day and night with her...She had hope again. Faith. Faith in him, faith in them.

They *would* survive this extremely painful low point in their lives. And while the future may not be better than what they'd had before—nothing could be better than when they'd had Cody in their lives—they would be together, and they would find a reason to smile again. The knowledge washed over her in waves, and a sense of rightness rushed in.

Thank You, Lord, for being here with us, for blessing us and our marriage. Thank You that Joe is opening up to me. I pray that when this trip is over, he'll come home with me again.

****

Joe awoke with a feeling of dread clutching his heart. He'd only meant to hold Lisa for a little while, just until she'd fallen asleep. Then he wanted to hold her just a little while longer, until he was ready to let go. But he'd fallen asleep himself and slept quite soundly for the first time since the accident.

Not wanting to stop and ponder the meaning in that, he gently eased Lisa out of his arms then climbed out of bed. When she didn't stir, he had to wonder if she was awake. That possibility was the only thing that kept him from leaning over and kissing her forehead.

Walk away now, his gut screamed. Just because she seemed peaceful and content now, didn't mean everything would be OK. The heartache he caused her would never end, and he couldn't—wouldn't—put her through any more pain.

To let her think anything different would be cruel. Joe had to distance himself now before any more damage was done to her heart. He could renew his walk with the Lord without renewing his relationship with her, couldn't he?

He studied her for a moment, wanting to commit her peaceful expression to memory. She still wore the sweatshirt they'd both cried over last night, pulled over the blue dress she'd worn to dinner. He didn't claim to know a lot about women, but he knew they valued comfort. He didn't see how Lisa could possibly be comfortable.

And yet she slept.

Hair tousled around her face, cheeks pink, it took a strength Joe didn't know he had in order to walk away. Before he could change his mind, he grabbed his shaving kit and headed into the bathroom.

Sadness twinged his soul as he showered and shaved. Somehow, he had to get through the day without being drawn closer to Lisa. Today, they would take Brandon and Chad on the seaplane, and while he'd been so excited about it before, now all he could think about was how good it felt to hold Lisa in his arms. The comfort she offered...he wanted more of it.

Somehow, he'd have to find the strength to do what was right. With so many other people around, it should be easy enough to distance himself from her. At least, that's what he thought until his eye caught the neat little row of Lisa's personal care items lined up on the bathroom counter. He picked up a bottle that said something about soft and manageable curls and sniffed. It smelled like her. Setting it back in place next to all of the other containers, Joe studied each of them. What would happen after their day in Juneau was over? Their cabin on this ship certainly wasn't big enough to allow him any distance.

****

After Lisa showered and dressed, she came out of the bathroom to find Joe typing away at his computer. Seeing him so focused on the computer screen gave her a momentary sense of panic. Had he changed his mind? No. It was her nerves talking, trying to take her focus off of the plane ride. But no matter what, she was going. She'd much rather risk her life on the seaplane than risk losing Joe all over again.

"What are you doing?" she asked.

Joe looked up at her and smiled, and her worries drained away. This was not the smile of a man who was shutting back down.

"Just checking my e-mail."

"E-mail? How can you check your e-mail? I don't even have cell phone reception."

"My carrier is better than yours?"

Now it was Lisa's turn to smile. She couldn't help it. Joe was teasing her. It was almost like old times.

"You know Mike. He always keeps us up on the latest technology." He explained how the connection would work from almost any location.

"Can I use it to send Rose an e-mail? I've tried a couple of times to call her but, as I said, I have no reception."

"Sure. But can it wait until tonight?" Joe shut the laptop and gave her a wide, enthusiastic smile. "Don't we have somewhere to be?"

"Right." Lisa slapped her forehead and tried to use humor to cover the nerves that just descended upon her. "The seaplane. How could I forget?"

Joe grabbed their jackets and held the door open for her. "I received an e-mail from Mike's secretary, Jennifer."

Cody's Sunday school teacher.

Lisa's breath caught in her throat.

"She told me about something that happened at church on Sunday morning." Joe gestured toward the door with a smile that could have earned him a spot on a toothpaste commercial. Curious, Lisa followed his lead toward the elevator.

"They had a special visitor at church," he said. "It was Rose."

"Rose? Really?"

Joe nodded and tears filled Lisa's eyes as she absorbed this information. Rose went to church. That meant her friend had been listening, even when she pretended otherwise. First Joe, and now Rose.

Miracles were happening all around her.

****

As they approached the docks where the brightly colored seaplanes were lined up in neat little rows of red, yellow, and blue, Lisa gulped. The cold chill indicated that her nerves kicked up a notch, and she shivered.

An engine roared to life as one of the planes prepared to take off. It sounded like a bucket of bolts trying to rattle loose. Lisa had visions of it falling out of the sky. A death trap if there ever was one. She didn't want to be in one when it decided to break apart and scatter all over the landscape.

"I—I—" Her knees turned to jelly, and she couldn't move her feet no matter how hard she tried. "Joe, I don't think—why don't you all go without me."

"But, Miss Lisa," Brandon wailed in protest. "You were going to sit by me."

"I don't think I can get on that thing." Much as she tried to keep the fear from her voice, she couldn't.

"It'll be fun." Though Brandon's smile was usually infectious, today it really didn't help Lisa feel any better.

"Yeah, it'll be fun." Joe's sweet-talking soft tone was one that sent shivers up her neck. He was trying to manipulate her, but it wouldn't work. He pointed to a wooden bench just off the sidewalk.

"Look, why don't you and Brandon sit here while we wait for Jessica. Chad and I are going to step over here and have a little chat."

Lisa watched with interest as Chad and Joe walked to the edge of the first dock, her nerves temporarily forgotten. They weren't facing her, but she could tell their conversation was intense.

"What do you think they're talking about?" Brandon asked.

"I don't know, honey. Probably something about the plane ride."

"Do you think my dad is going to change his mind, and I won't get to go?" His blue eyes were wide, his brow furrowed. He was much too young to wrinkle his forehead like that.

She kissed Brandon's forehead and smoothed her thumbs across his brow. "Don't you worry one little bit, Brandon. We're going on that plane."

"We certainly are." Jessica approached wearing blue jeans, a bright red sweatshirt, and a huge smile. "What are we waiting for?"

"We were starting to worry about you," Lisa told her.

"Not me, Miss Jessica. I knew you'd be here!"

Jessica smiled at Brandon with so much love, Lisa found herself wondering what it must be like for such a loving woman to have never had children. "I wouldn't miss it for the world. I just got lost in the shuffle. Now what's taking those guys so long?"

"My dad and Mr. Joe are having a little chat." Brandon said it in almost the exact tone Joe had, and Lisa had to smother a laugh.

Jessica gave her a questioning glance over the top of Brandon's head, but Lisa just shrugged.

"What's 'the shuffle'?"

This time Lisa did laugh while Jessica explained to Brandon about the crowd.

Chad and Joe slowly walked back, looking serious. Too serious. What had just transpired? She tensed as they approached, worried that Chad was furious and would take Brandon back to the boat.

"Let's go." Joe spoke quietly. "We have a seaplane to catch."

Lisa was so relieved for Brandon she almost forgot her nerves. Until she stepped onto the wooden dock and caught a strong whiff of fuel.

The sound of a blue seaplane leaving the dock vibrated up through the wood beams and the fuel smell was even stronger. She could see Joe's mouth moving but couldn't hear.

"What?"

"That's our plane over there." Joe shouted and pointed at the red plane parked at the end of the dock.

"Thanks for pointing that out," she said wryly as they approached the bucket of bolts. She slowed her pace, dragging her heels like a captive walking the plank off the end of a pirate ship.

Brandon grabbed her hand in a sudden movement as if he knew her thoughts. "My dad said we might get to see the whales today." Brandon beamed and his eyes sparkled with hope.

While that should have been all she needed to bound eagerly toward the end of the dock, Lisa continued to walk as slowly as possible.

"Just think of it as sightseeing from the sky," Jessica said. "They assured me it's a great way to see the Misty Fjords. And we might even see a bear or two along with Brandon's whales."

Lisa's eyes widened and she stared at Jessica. "Aren't you afraid?"

"Not at all. But I don't blame you for being scared. I've never flown before, but I'm not going to let it stop me from seeing all of this from the air." She waved her arms around to indicate the glaciers, mountains, and water. "Are you, Lisa?"

"I—I don't know." Once again, fear threatened to paralyze her.

Please, dear Lord, wipe that concerned look off Joe's face. Her prayer wasn't answered, and Lisa found herself torn between wanting to make Joe happy and keeping both feet on the ground.

"God, please give me strength," she muttered as she took a step toward the seaplane. Her mouth went dry as Joe waited patiently. The pilot looked irritated as her feet seemed to grow roots right into the dock.

"Please, Miss Lisa," Brandon begged.

Joe stepped in front of her and held out his hand. "Please, Miss Lisa?" He echoed little Brandon with an eagerness Lisa couldn't ignore. This was something he really wanted. She found herself putting her hand in Joe's, and before she knew it, she was standing on the dock in front of the bright red seaplane.

"Come on, Lisa," Jessica called from halfway up the steps where the pilot now assisted her. "If I can venture out on my own after all these years, surely you can step on this bird. You don't want to disappoint your handsome husband, do you?"

Lisa looked into Joe's eager brown eyes then down at their hands clasped together. The dock bounced under her feet. The smell of saltwater tickled her nose. She did not want to leave this earth.

Joe smiled then, a simple encouraging smile, and

gestured toward the plane.

Reluctant, dread making her feet feel like cement blocks, she took one tentative step all the while looking at Joe. His smile lit his eyes, and Lisa's feet were a tiny bit lighter as she took yet another step. *Keep your eyes on Joe. You can do it.*

The pounding of her heart hammered in her chest, and she could scarcely catch her breath. As much as she wanted to attribute it to her husband's handsome face and the fact that he held his hand out to her, she couldn't. It was fear. Plain, simple fear.

"I—can't," she whispered thickly as she approached the plane.

"Sure you can," Jessica declared.

"No, I can't. You go without me."

Joe, bless him, didn't say a word. But she did see the light in his eyes dim just a smidgen. He wanted this so badly. How could she disappoint him after all they'd been through? It was such a small thing to ask.

She took one more step and was immediately in front of the plane.

"We about ready?" the pilot grumbled.

Lisa ignored his sarcastic manner as Joe helped her up the steps. She stopped in the doorway and glanced around. Three faces stared at her. Jessica, Brandon, and Chad. Sardines in a tin can. She didn't want to be one, too.

Chad and Jessica sat in the seats directly behind the pilot, each by a window with an empty seat between them.

Directly behind his father, with two empty seats next to him, sat Brandon. He patted the seat beside him. "C'mon, Miss Lisa. Sit here. Unless you wanna sit by a window, too."

Lisa couldn't suppress a shudder. When her feet finally obeyed, she had to bend her head forward and climb past Jessica to get to her own seat. The plane smelled musty, and she fought the urge to gag.

"I'll sit in the middle," she muttered and somehow managed to shuffle toward her seat. She was relieved when Joe took his seat next to her. He offered his hand to her again, and she grabbed onto it without hesitation. His grip was warm and firm, and Lisa wanted to melt into him. He must have sensed it because he let go of her hand before she could react and wrapped his arm across her shoulder. He pulled her tight then reached over with his other arm and clasped her hand once again. Relief coursed through her. There was no way she could do this by herself. But with Joe next to her, she was safe and loved and could overcome anything.

"You OK?" His breath, warm against her ear, skittered down her neck.

With him holding her, she was more than OK. She could do this. For him. Trying to hide her hesitation, she nodded.

Brandon patted her hand as if he was trying to be a grownup and offer her some comfort. "I'm glad you're here."

Not wanting to let him down, Lisa tried to smile.

All of a sudden, the engines shut off and a deafening silence rang through the small plane. Lisa took a deep breath and let it out. They weren't going.

Oh, thank You, Lord.

She started to stand.

"You folks sit tight. Ralph, over there, is having some engine trouble. I'm gonna help him out, and then we'll be on our way. Sorry for the delay, but around here we try to help each other out as much as possible."

"As it should be," Jessica piped up.

The pilot grinned at Jessica before he dipped his head and climbed out of the plane. A red stain spread up her neck. Her face was probably as red, but Lisa couldn't tell for sure. For some reason, Jessica wouldn't turn around.

"How long do you think it'll take, Dad? I'm bored."

"Hey, Brandon." Joe leaned across Lisa for a moment. "How about I tell you a story?"

"That'd be great!"

Brandon listened intently while Joe told him a story about a boy who lived in a mining camp with his little donkey during the California gold rush. The tale was one Lisa recognized. Joe used to tell it to Cody. While part of her wanted to cry, the other part was content to lean her head against Joe's chest and listen to the rumble of his voice as he told the story.

When he got to the end, Brandon tapped his dad on the shoulder.

"Hey, Dad. I liked that story. Do you think we can buy that book when we get home?"

"Sure, Brandon." Chad turned to Joe "What's the name of the book?"

"Well..." Joe shifted uncomfortably and looked over Brandon's head and out the window. "It doesn't really have a name. It's...I made it up."

Lisa sat straight up in her seat and stared at Joe. "Joseph Kendall, are you kidding me?"

He pressed his lips together and shook his head.

"You made up that story?"

He nodded.

"What about the other stories you used to tell Cody, with the same little boy and his donkey?"

Again he nodded, but a small smile began to lift the corners of his mouth.

"And why is it I'm just now hearing about this?"

Looking suddenly shy, Joe shrugged.

Lisa shook her head. "I had no idea. Did Cody know you made these stories up?"

Sadness washed over his features as he nodded. Lisa squeezed his hand, wishing there was something she could do to take away his pain.

"You should make them into a book so my dad can buy them for me." Brandon bounced on his seat then tapped his dad on the shoulder again. "Right, Dad? You'll buy it for me, won't you?"

Though he didn't turn around, Chad nodded his head.

Jessica turned to look at Joe. "You really should write them down."

"OK." The pilot settled back into his seat, having somehow boarded the plane with no one noticing. "You folks ready to take off?" Without waiting for an answer, he started the engine. "Buckle up," he shouted over the roar.

Fear invaded Lisa's nerves again, and her stomach took a dangerous dip. Joe pulled her close once more, and the edges of her fear seeped away. She looked up to see Jessica watching them, a trace of a smile on her face. Almost like…satisfaction. Like she was rooting for them.

Jessica had promised to pray for her, and Lisa couldn't help but smile at the thought. With her prayers and Jessica's prayers, Joe didn't stand a chance.

The small plane began to pull away from the dock.

As they slowly glided over the water, picking up speed before lifting into the air, Joe must have sensed her panic because he laced his fingers through hers and kissed the top of her head. Then he pulled her closer, and she buried her face in his chest, embarrassed to realize tears leaked from her eyes and ran down her face.

"It'll be OK," Joe whispered as he continued to hold her tight. After what seemed like hours, the edges of fear slowly seeped away again. This time, she prayed it wouldn't return.

Finally, she lifted her head and looked up at Joe. "Thank you," she whispered.

"Are you OK?"

Grateful he cared, she tried to smile. Her facial muscles were frozen, so she feared it came out more as a grimace. "If anything happens, we're over the water, and these big rudders should break our fall. If the truth is anything different, I don't want to know about it."

Joe laughed and it zinged its way to the center of her heart. What an awesome sound. *Lord, please let this keep happening until it becomes natural again.* Her prayer was answered several times during the plane ride as Brandon kept them entertained. Though she never totally relaxed, Lisa's hope was once again in full bloom. Sitting here with Joe, privileged to see stunningly breathtaking views, the only thing that kept it from perfection was Cody's absence.

Lisa's eyes misted over when she saw some brown bears on a mountainside, but as the plane nosed down to return to the dock, they threatened to become full-blown tears.

They hadn't seen any whales. No sign of them anywhere.

"I can't believe this." Lisa willed herself not to cry. "Every single person I've ever known who has taken an Alaskan cruise has seen the orcas. Why can't we?"

"I'm sorry, Lisa."

"Don't be." Lisa blinked back more tears and tried to smile, but the lump that filled her throat made it impossible. "It's just the way it is. I'm sure there's a reason, but I don't know what it could be."

Joe helped her down the steps of the little plane and held her close as they made their way down the dock and toward the center of Juneau. Brandon and Chad were ahead of them, and Jessica was still talking to the pilot.

"Don't worry, Lisa." He squeezed her hand. "We'll see them before we go home. I'm sure of it."

We. Home.

Had she heard him right? Yes, Joe really said *we*, but did he mean it the way she took it?

Dare she even hope?

Lisa looked up and Joe smiled.

Yes, she dared.

17

"It was a wonderful day." Lisa leaned against the wall in the elevator and sighed with exhaustion. Though she was tired, it was the good type of tired, like being at the beach or an amusement park all day. The hope she'd tried to suppress earlier was bigger than the lump choking her throat.

They'd been together. They didn't see the whales. She'd been scared to death of the plane, but she learned something new about Joe, and he'd mentioned home. It was hard not to hope when Joe said *we* and *home* in the same breath and by the time they'd arrived back at the ship after touring the cute little fishing town, her hope grew ever more intense. Had he meant the home they used to share together? Or the office he slept in? She wanted to ask, but, of course, she didn't.

"You enjoyed yourself even though you were up in the air in a bucket of bolts?" Joe threw her a smile and pressed the button for the Denali Deck. Her heart warmed at the sight. She smiled back, infused with a happy glow.

"The view from that sardine can was nothing next to learning about your children's stories. I never knew." A hint of a blush crept into his cheeks. She wouldn't let his embarrassment stop her from giving him encouragement. "You should put them down on paper and send them to a publisher."

"I don't know, Lisa. Not having Cody to tell them

to takes the joy out of it. I made them up for *him.*"

"But you told the story to Brandon without any hesitation. Maybe over time, that joy will come back to you." A look crossed his face that told her now wasn't a good time to continue this conversation. "I've been dying to ask what you said to Chad."

Joe shrugged. "I just talked to him about the other night at dinner. I told him that while it was really none of my business what he did with his son, I let him know how difficult it had been to listen to him talk to Brandon the way he did while you and I are grieving for Cody." He looked at her, his eyes bright with what Lisa suspected were unshed tears.

"Brandon's a bright, charming kid. I suggested that Chad cherish every moment he has with his son—nothing he didn't already know. He's still grieving his wife's death. I just thought a reminder might be worthwhile." Joe looked away and Lisa sensed he was losing the battle with the tears. Her suspicion was confirmed when she heard a muffled sniffle, so she didn't press him for any more details.

When they stepped out of the elevator and headed toward their room, she caught sight of the solarium. Right now, it offered a unique view of Juneau in the evening. She soaked it in, determined never to forget the day they'd spent together.

Joe stood beside her as she took in the sight. "Cody would have loved this."

He'd mentioned their son in such an easy manner.

"I'm not so sure," Lisa said slowly. "He would have been sad about not seeing the whales."

Beside her, Joe took a deep breath then slowly let it out. "You're probably right." He reached out and clasped her hand. "Are you feeling better about not seeing them?"

She looked down at their joined hands. "I'm doing better." Even as she spoke, she tried to mean it.

"Like I said, we'll see them before we go home."

There they were again. Those two little words, packed with so much meaning. Some cynical part of her brain tried to tell her she was grasping at straws, but she didn't believe it. God was smiling on them. He had to be.

"And another thing." Joe interrupted her thoughts before she could think any more about it. "Cody would have loved exploring the ship like Brandon has."

"I'm sure they would have been fast friends."

"Cody always did make friends easily."

Lisa nodded and forced the tears to stay put. She stayed quiet as she followed Joe down the hall to their room. Once inside, she walked to the closet.

"I have something to show you," she called over her shoulder. She dug in her suitcase, searching for the wind chimes she'd bought in the gift store. When she finally found it, she unwrapped them to show Joe. "I bought them the other day. Right before I missed seeing the whales. They remind me of Cody."

"They're nice, Lisa." Joe rose from the lumpy green chair and took them from her. Then he went over to the bunk beds and hung them on the bedframe near her pillow so she'd see them before she went to sleep and again when she woke up.

"Thank you, Joe." She was pleased that he understood how important they were to her. She stretched out on Joe's bunk instead of settling in one of the lumpy chairs as he'd done. She hoped he didn't mind, but she didn't have the energy to climb up the ladder right now.

"I'm sorry." Joe startled her when he broke the long silence. "I shouldn't have mentioned him."

"Yes. You should. We *need* to talk about him. It's part of how we heal."

"I don't deserve to heal."

Lisa sucked in a breath. Joe blamed himself for not being there, even though she'd never heard him come right out and say it. Did he think the accident wouldn't have happened if he'd been there? She'd always had the feeling that's what he believed. She recognized the blame in his eyes—because the very same blame reflected in her heart.

She rolled over on her side and stared at her husband. "Yes, you do deserve to heal, Joe. You didn't do anything wrong."

"Yes, I did. I wasn't there. I was never there."

"You didn't cause the accident." She swallowed hard and sat up, unable to let him suffer any longer. This matter needed to be cleared up right now. Far too much time had passed without this conversation. Lisa only hoped Joe wouldn't hate her afterward.

"I caused it." Lisa's hands trembled as she watched for Joe's reaction. "It's my fault. So stop torturing yourself." Her voice rose to a pitch that made her cringe. Scared as she was of his reaction, she couldn't let him blame himself any longer.

"I killed our son." Her words hung in the air. She wished she could call them back, wished she could change the look of shock and hurt on Joe's face.

"No, Lisa." He rose from his chair and came to kneel in front of her.

"I put off telling you, because I didn't want you to hate me. Then you stopped coming home, and the opportunity was lost. But now I see exactly how you've punished yourself, and I can't let it continue. Joe, it wasn't your fault. Hate me instead."

"I could never hate you." His tone was so gentle that hot tears swelled over, burning her eyes as they fell. "Is that why you've lost so much weight? Did you stop eating right because you blame yourself?"

Swiping at the tears, Lisa bit back her denial. They'd discussed this before, and she'd managed to skirt the issue. She didn't want to rehash it now, but maybe she had no choice.

There were things that only she and God knew. Part of it *did* have to do with her not eating right, and maybe now was the time to tell Joe. But first, she needed to make Joe see that the blame lay at her feet. Not his, and not Rose's husband.

"I know I should have told you this at the beginning. But I was so—devastated. At first, I didn't realize you were blaming yourself. If I did, I would have told you right away. I never wanted you to suffer." Her voice broke, and Joe reached out and stroked her arm.

Lisa should have taken comfort from the warmth of his contact, but she couldn't. There was too much to tell him, and when she finished he really would hate her. Abruptly, she pulled away from Joe's touch and, lying down, she rolled over to face the wall. She couldn't look at him while she did this. It was hard enough to say without seeing recrimination in his eyes.

"Joe, I wasn't paying attention that day. Yes, Rose's husband ran the red light. There's no question about that. But I was upset, and in a rush to get to the game. The instant the light turned green, I hit the gas." She stopped and took a deep breath. "I hate myself." The bitterness shocked her and drained her even further. There was so much more to tell him, she wasn't sure where she'd get the strength.

"Lisa." Joe spoke gently. "Don't do this to yourself."

The edge of the bed dipped and creaked as Joe sat on it. He touched her back, his fingers light and warm. Still, she continued to face the wall.

"I don't hate you," Joe said after a while. "I'm not so sure I hate myself, either. I thought I did, but...talking with God again...I just don't think I do."

"There's more, though, Joe." Lisa swallowed hard and wished she could call the words back. Joe remained silent, merely waiting for her to continue. Lisa was so scared of what his reaction would be after she told him, that she could hear the blood pounding through her veins.

She pressed her hand to abdomen. Telling him would be so hard. "It's about that last weekend we spent together," she whispered.

"Your birthday?"

"I should have told you, but when you stopped coming home—"

"I'm sorry, Lisa."

Still facing the wall, Lisa nodded. "I am, too. If I had known, I would have taken better care of myself." Tears burned her eyes and spilled down her face. Guilt churned deep within.

Behind her, Joe sucked in a sharp breath and pulled his hand from her back. "Lisa, were you...did we make a baby that weekend?"

Lisa bit her lip and tried to hold back the sobs, but they overcame her, and she couldn't answer. Joe's arms were around her then, his legs beside hers. He stretched out then pulled her close. Feelings swirled around her, and if not for the guilt, she would have reveled in them.

"Why didn't you tell me?" His gentle, concerned tone brushed against her heart, and she was warmed by the fact that it wasn't accusatory.

"By the time I knew for sure, you'd already stopped coming home. I didn't want it to be the reason you came back to me."

"Aw, Lisa." He gently turned her in his arms and pressed his forehead to hers. "You went through so much on your own. I'd give anything if I could take it all back."

His broken whisper tore at her heart, and Lisa squeezed her eyes shut, unable to look at him. "Our baby died, Joe." A lump of pain squeezed her throat making it difficult to speak. Still, she had to say it. "Because of me. Because I didn't take care of myself."

"Lisa, look at me." His fingers brushed lightly against her cheeks before finding their way under her chin and tilting it up. Hesitantly, she opened her eyes even though tears continued to spill down her face.

There was no mistaking the love in Joe's eyes as he gazed at her. Tears tracked down his face, too, and he made no move to hide them.

"It's not your fault." His voice was hoarse, broken. "Let's stop blaming ourselves."

Lisa pressed her face against his chest, and he tightened his hold on her, pulling her close as she let the pain flow from the depths of her soul. When she finished crying, she prayed silently and asked the Lord to lift the guilt from both their hearts.

Hours later, when Lisa woke, Joe slept softly beside her. A quiet peace lifted her soul, warming her heart. If Joe had been awake, she would have rejoiced out loud. This was the peace that vanished from her months ago—the peace she thought she'd lost forever. The peace that let her know the Lord was nearby and that filled up the dark empty spots in her soul.

Could it be because she'd blocked Him out by bottling up her guilt? She'd prayed for Joe, prayed for herself, prayed for peace. But until now, she'd never really given her feelings of guilt to the Lord.

Thank you, Lord. You really are here with me. You didn't leave me after all.

As she lay in Joe's arms, Lisa prayed he'd wake up with the same peace flowing through him that she basked in right now.

****

What was happening to him?

After all of the emotion of last night, Joe awoke the next morning feeling renewed and looking forward to the day in Skagway. The sound of the shower running came from inside the small bathroom. Lisa was getting ready for their day trip. He hoped she hadn't changed her mind. Somehow, he didn't think she had. In spite of the newfound knowledge that she'd suffered through a miscarriage alone, a sense of peace settled over him.

Thank you, Lord, for continuing to reach for me. I know I don't deserve it.

Joe stopped praying for a moment so he could think about it. He didn't deserve God's peace. No one did. The good news was the Lord was a God of grace and mercy. He gave His peace freely to anyone who asked.

A deep cleansing breath left him humble and filled

with thanksgiving. "I know I let Lisa down, Lord, and she suffered because I abandoned her. Forgive me. Please help me make it up to her."

Something shifted inside him and Joe realized he wasn't trying to push the joy away. His enormous burden of guilt had lifted and it felt so amazingly good.

Looking back over the last several days, Joe recalled his hopelessness when Lisa first arrived on the ship. God had sent her to him so he could find his way back. Back to the Lord, back to her. All he had to do was tell her. Then perhaps the two of them could begin to heal.

If it wasn't too late, he wanted them to heal together, with the Lord firmly at the center of their lives.

****

The tour in Skagway would take an entire day, so Joe and Lisa departed the ship before breakfast. Instead, they ate on a sightseeing train as it took them up the mountains to the gold mines and nearby historic campgrounds. Joe was glad Lisa brought her camera along.

Brandon and his father were on the train, accompanied by Jessica, but they were seated several rows back.

Joe looked forward to panning for gold and, in spite of her red, puffy eyes, Lisa seemed to practically dance with excitement. It was then that Joe realized Lisa had been infused with the same sense of peace he had. Their healing had begun.

Did letting go of his guilt mean saying good-bye to

his son? Should he use this time as a tribute to his Cody? Maybe he would make up one last story as his way of saying good-bye to his little boy.

The stray thought was unwelcome, and he quickly dismissed it. He was *not* ready to say good-bye to Cody. Not yet. Please God, not yet. It hurts way too much.

"Joe?" Lisa's voice cut into his thoughts. "Are you all right?"

He nodded.

"We don't have to do this, you know."

"I know. I"—he swallowed hard as his voice broke—"I want to." As hard as it would be to walk through the historic gold camps without his son, he still needed to do it.

Lisa smiled up at him, one of those smiles that never failed to pull at his heart. She wore a pale blue fleece jacket that highlighted the blue in her red-rimmed eyes. Unable to help himself, he planted a light kiss on her forehead. He wanted to continue down to her lips, but Jessica was staring at them from several seats back with a knowing look on her face. He tried to avoid her grandmotherly gaze and realized he didn't really want to. He needed people in his life. He'd made a terrible mistake when he chose to isolate himself. He smiled at Jessica and this time the smile was genuine.

Perhaps there was hope for him after all.

****

Lisa could tell things had changed as much for Joe as they had for her. The longing in his eyes mirrored the longing in her heart. But something still seemed to bother him. The closer they drew to the gold mining camps, the more Joe appeared to grow pensive. He was probably thinking of Cody.

Be with him, Lord. Help this be a good day for him.

Afraid she'd be bored touring the gold mine camps, Lisa was happy to find she enjoyed herself. From time to time they came across Brandon and Chad—who were accompanied by Jessica. Brandon, in all of his little-boy-enthusiasm, kept trying to follow Lisa and Joe. But Jessica consistently managed to intervene, for which Lisa was grateful.

The surrounding mountains and woods were magnificent, the history lesson fascinating, and the way Joe kept muttering to himself as they wandered the site was positively intriguing. What was going on in that head of his? He seemed interested in their surroundings and it certainly appeared to take his mind off his troubles. He no longer seemed to be fighting to keep from letting down his guard.

The sites were either well-preserved and well-cared for or perfectly recreated. Not being a historian, Lisa wasn't sure which. But it didn't matter because she loved it.

Joe did, too, apparently. Looking quite pleased with himself and still muttering, he hovered over everything for excruciatingly long periods. Still, he was smiling and that was all Lisa cared about.

She loved him. And he loved her.

Even though he had yet to commit to it, it was only a matter of time before Joe was back where he belonged.

After the tour of the gold mines, they ate lunch at a rustic old log-hewn inn. It was part of the tour package, along with a hike in the woods and fishing at the lake.

Brandon managed to coerce his father and Jessica into joining Lisa and Joe for lunch, but he knew about the lake—and the fishing poles—at the end of the trail and grew antsier by the minute.

"It's time to go on the hike, Miss Lisa." Brandon practically jumped out of his chair, potato chip crumbs falling from his shirt and spotting his chin.

Lisa instinctively reached for a napkin to brush them away as she'd done so many times for Cody. "Brandon, honey, I'm going to skip the hike today. But you go along with your dad and Miss Jessica. You'll have fun, I promise. You might even catch a big fish."

She turned to Joe. "Is it okay if we skip the hike?" She held her breath, waiting for his answer, praying it would be a yes.

He nodded, but there was a hint of a promise in his eyes. Hope spread across Lisa's chest and she couldn't help but smile.

The inn was warm and toasty and she planned to suggest they use the time together to write down some of his stories. The morning at the mines and camps might have given him some new ideas they could brainstorm.

Excited about this new side of Joe, Lisa wanted to help him develop his ideas as much as possible.

"Can we stay with you, Miss Lisa?" The pleading in Brandon's eyes tugged at her and she hesitated, torn between wanting to be alone with Joe and not wanting to disappoint this sweet boy.

Jessica glanced at Lisa and raised one eyebrow. Then she turned to Brandon. "Sweetheart, I think Lisa and Joe need some time together."

A pout clouded Brandon's usual sunny disposition.

"I'm sure they'll be happy to sit with you on the train on the way back," Jessica said.

"We will, Brandon," Lisa said. "I promise. But right now, Joe and I are just going to talk. You'll be bored if you stayed here with us. Hiking with Jessica and your dad will be a lot more fun."

"No it won't. It'll be boring with them, too."

"Actually, I don't think it will." Jessica pressed her lips into a secretive smile and lowered her lashes. "Unless you count fishing as boring."

"Fishing? Really?" The corners of Brandon's lips turned up, and he no longer sounded upset. "Can we, Dad? Can we?"

Lisa breathed a sigh of relief then smiled at Jessica in thanks. Jessica winked at her in return. Clearly, Brandon didn't remember his previous declaration about not liking fish. Maybe there was a difference between catching fish and eating them, at least in a little boy's mind.

After the small group departed with their guides, the couple who ran the inn, Millie and Paul, was most accommodating and seemed happy to host Lisa and Joe for the afternoon.

Millie, a sweet-natured woman with a round face and snow white hair, helped them get settled in a spacious room that had a fireplace on each end. While they made themselves at home on an overstuffed leather couch, Millie brought them hot chocolate and a plate of cookies. Lisa smiled as Joe dug into the cookies, happy to see him enjoy something. So far this day had been truly blessed in that area.

When Joe had devoured the last of the cookies, Lisa pulled his laptop out of her backpack.

"Are you kidding?" Joe stared at the laptop.

"You've been carrying that thing around all day?"

"It's not that heavy. Besides, I figured you might come up with a new story idea while we were at the gold camp. This way you could write it down so you won't forget it."

"Wow, Lisa. I don't know what to say."

"Say yes."

"Yes."

Then he shocked her by leaning over and kissing her on the forehead. When he leaned back in his chair, his smile was wide, and his brown eyes sparkled. Warm and toasty, Lisa was quite certain it had nothing to do with the fireplace.

18

Joe blamed it on the fire.

Sitting on an overstuffed leather couch near the fireplace with the taste of hot chocolate and marshmallows on his tongue, he huddled with Lisa, brainstorming a children's story idea.

Now, as Lisa typed ideas into his laptop and fired random thoughts at him, her cheeks flushed a rosy shade that seemed to add light to her already bright blue eyes. A warmth curled around his heart that left Joe feeling...well...romantic.

He couldn't believe how passionate she was about his children's stories or that she'd been lugging his laptop around in her backpack all day. Granted, it was a lightweight model. But still, her enthusiasm for his story ideas warmed him more than the fire and hot chocolate ever could.

Would he still feel this way without the fire crackling in front of them?

Yes. The answer came to him in a flash. He could be standing outside barefoot with no jacket in the wilds of Alaska, and he'd feel the same way.

The urge to kiss her was overpowering. He leaned toward her, studying her face. Her eyes, bright from the reflection of the fire, widened. Her face seemed to soften, as if she knew of his intention.

"Lisa," he whispered. He leaned closer, but she put her palm out and sat up straight.

"Joe, there's still something I need to tell you about."

He groaned and sat back. She sounded so serious. He didn't want to have a heavy conversation. "Let's not talk right now."

"We have to. Much as I want to kiss you, I can't until we talk about this." Her face pinched with worry, and she swallowed hard.

"Lisa, we've already talked about the accident. And the..." He hesitated because it hurt him to even say it, and he knew how much it hurt her as well. "And the baby. You're not to blame. So we don't need to do anything but enjoy the moment."

"I lied to you," she blurted out.

Lisa was the most honest person he knew. He couldn't imagine her lying about anything. At a loss for what it could be, he motioned with his hand for her to continue. "About...?"

"You were right all along." She muttered and looked down at her lap as if ashamed to make eye contact.

What was he right about? He recalled their last several conversations, and the answer came to him in a flash.

"Your reason for being here?"

Biting her lower lip, she nodded.

"I see."

"It was exactly what you said. I hoped to get you to come home."

He should be mad. If she'd told him yesterday, he might have been. But this was a new day. He was a new man. This was his opening.

"You don't look angry." Surprise lilted in her voice.

"I suspected."

A picture of his son came into his mind, Cody's eyes bright blue like Lisa's, his eager, happy smile.

Joe knew then, Cody would want his parents to be together like they were at this moment. But he wouldn't want it to be a fleeting moment. He'd want it to be forever. Joe did, too. And he didn't feel panic, sadness, or guilt. Instead, he felt warmth and love, and the need to fix things.

Was it even possible? *Yes.* The love of the Lord surrounded him, filling him with peace and hope.

Before he could take the thought any further, the large double doors burst open and the group of hikers burst in, little Brandon proudly leading the way.

"Mr. Joe! We had the best-est time. You should have been with us."

Joe looked at Brandon's father who stood behind the boy, looking weary but content. Chad must have finally allowed himself to relax enough to enjoy his son. Joe was glad.

"That's great Brandon. But I had a good time, too. I needed to stay here and take care of some things." He looked over at Lisa and smiled. He wasn't done taking care of things, and as soon as they were alone together, he'd make things right once and for all and hope she'd forgive him for even entertaining the thought of a divorce.

Brandon was at his side shaking his arm before he could even blink. "You gotta come, Mr. Joe. Please. You gotta see all the fishes I caught."

One look into that small but earnest face made it impossible to say no.

He turned to Lisa. "Do you mind? I won't be gone long."

"I'd be upset if you didn't." The smile on her face warmed his heart as he followed Brandon and his father back out the door.

19

While Lisa waited for Joe to return, she settled on the couch and decided to send Rose an e-mail. She had so much to tell her friend about how much progress she and Joe had made.

After the computer booted back up, Lisa clicked the icon for the e-mail program. Joe's inbox appeared and she was just about to select "compose" when something caught her eye. Something ugly that caused her heart to skip a beat. The subject line of an e-mail in the inbox. *Re: The Divorce.*

OK, that shouldn't necessarily give her pause. She willed her nerves to be still. Joe was a divorce lawyer, after all. It was probably from a client. She searched for the sender's name, and her heart sank. It was from Mike Lee.

She tried to tell herself that it didn't mean anything, but all she had to do was scan the contents of the inbox to see the subject lines that pertained to his work.

Re: Case #60582 or *FWD: JD vs. KD.*

Since Joe handled many divorces, he would never send out an e-mail simply titled *The Divorce.*

Lisa's hand trembled as she moved her finger over the touchpad but nothing compared to the trembling that started in her knees and rumbled up to her throat.

Should she open it? What if it was about her and Joe? Did she really want to know?

She rubbed her finger over the touchpad and a tiny white arrow jerked across the computer screen before landing on its intended spot.

Re: The divorce.

Eyes squeezed shut, Lisa clicked to open the e-mail. She didn't want to see the contents, did she? Of course not. But at the same time, she couldn't not look.

Finally, daring to peek, Lisa looked at the body of the e-mail.

OK, Joe. It's a go.

That was it? That's all the e-mail said? There was nothing about her and Joe. Lisa breathed a sigh of relief and started to close the e-mail, but down at the bottom of the screen, she noticed there was more. The beginning section of the e-mail Mike replied to. The one from Joe. Lisa scrolled down, unable to keep from reading it.

Mike:

I know we've talked about it before, but that doesn't make it any easier.

I've decided to go ahead with the divorce.

Please file the papers as soon as possible. See you in two weeks.

Joe

No. No. No. No. No. No!

Lisa buried her face in her hands, feeling sick. Everything she'd worked for, hoped for, and prayed for. Done. Over with. Just like that.

Why, God? Why?

Joe was done with her. The last couple of days had been a lie.

We're supposed to find the joy in our sorrows, the blessings in the storm.

The words she'd spoken to Joe came back to haunt

her. She was supposed to look for blessings and joy. Where was she supposed to find them now?

Practice what you preach, Lisa, she told herself. *Live what you believe, even if you don't feel it, even if you feel like dying inside.*

The door burst open and Joe came in, a wide smile on his face. "That kid is something else. You should have seen all the fish he caught. They've headed back to the ship. Are you ready to g—" The smile faded from his lips.

Lisa couldn't speak. How could it all have been a lie? Unable to face him now, she got up and walked into the kitchen.

****

A sick sort of dread settled in Joe's stomach. Lisa hadn't even looked at him.

He crossed the room to follow her into the kitchen, but as he neared the table where the screen of his laptop glowed, he pulled up short. An e-mail, *the* e-mail, seemed to glare out at him like a beacon.

No! God, why did You let her see that?

His heart leaped when Lisa came back into the room. He had to explain.

"Lisa, I—"

She glared at him. "Time to get back to the ship, Joe." She walked out the door without another word.

Helpless despair washed over him as they returned to the ship. Once in their cabin, Lisa tossed her bag aside then climbed up the narrow ladder to the top bunk. Joe ducked as one shoe followed the other to the floor before she turned to face the wall.

Hoping and praying she would turn and talk to

him, Joe sat in the chair beside the bunk. But she remained silent—almost despondent—avoiding eye contact with him.

"Lisa, please." Did his voice sound as awkward to Lisa as it did to his own ears? "I'm sorry."

Lisa turned and speared him with a withering look.

"Really, if I could just explain?"

Lisa pressed her lips together and rolled back to face the wall.

"I didn't want a divorce, Lisa. I never did. I just didn't know what else to do. When Mike suggested it, the idea made sense. I thought you'd be better off without me. Things are different now, though. Please, let's talk about it."

But Joe's plea fell on deaf ears as Lisa continued to ignore him.

Determined to wait her out, he pulled a blanket from the bed and tried to get comfortable in the chair. Just as he was about to fall asleep, Lisa whispered, "The answer's no, by the way."

"No? What?" He straightened in confusion, feeling as if the hard back of the chair had permanently dented his back.

"The divorce." Her voice seemed to falter over the words. "I won't sign the papers."

"Lisa, there are no papers. There never were."

Joe waited for answer, for her to say more, so they could talk it out. But she remained silent after that. And as the room grew dark he sat pondering her declaration that she wouldn't sign the non-existent papers, wondering what the future might hold for them.

By morning, Joe was no closer to finding answers,

though every muscle in his body ached from sleeping in the hard chair.

At breakfast, Lisa was silent. Too silent.

He wanted to talk to her—to make her understand—but he was certain she still wouldn't listen.

He would try, though.

Please, Lord, help her to hear what's in my heart.

20

We're supposed to find the joy in our sorrows, the blessings in the storm.

The words came back to haunt Lisa once again. She still hadn't managed to come up with anything to feel joyful about or to find one single blessing.

It was Cody's birthday today, which made it all the more difficult to find anything to feel blessed about. Today was the day the entire trip was supposed to have centered around, the reason they bought the tickets in the first place.

Her little boy. Cody. He was supposed to be here with her, with Joe, the three of them together. Lisa wiped at her eyes with the back of her hand then put her fist to her mouth in an effort to suppress her sobs.

They were on a charter boat with about thirty other people, headed away from the cruise ship and toward Glacier Bay. Joe had planned the day for her prior to her finding his e-mail. He'd invited Jessica, Brandon, and Chad, and Lisa couldn't bring herself to disappoint Brandon by not showing up.

Luckily, the boat was large enough that no one could hear her cries and she could be alone with her thoughts.

She sat alone in an alcove off the main cabin where, she supposed, she could lick her wounds over Joe's plans for a divorce. She'd meant it when she said she wouldn't sign the papers, but she still wasn't sure what the future held for them if Joe truly didn't want to remain married to her.

Occasionally, she could hear Brandon firing questions at different people. Each time he did, Lisa tensed, waiting for Chad to scold him for bothering them. But he surprised her, often chiming in with questions of his own. Joe's talk with Chad really seemed to have had an impact on him.

There. A blessing stared her right in the face.

The thought brought her up short.

Brandon and Chad's relationship.

Restored.

All thanks to Joe.

Another thought occurred to her: When Joe had seen Cody's sweatshirt, he said he'd been able to picture Cody's face. Something he hadn't been able to do for a long time.

Another blessing.

Also, Joe was praying again. He'd bowed his head at dinner the other night. And he'd prayed other times, like when he couldn't find her after she'd missed seeing the whales.

Filled with silent amazement, Lisa stood and walked through the cabin and out to the back deck where she sat down on a bench that faced the water. She stared out at the boat's wake, at the smaller boats that seemed to disappear behind them. Then she looked at the snow-capped mountain peaks that towered above the trees.

A bittersweet mixture of joy and sorrow washed over her.

Joe was making his way back to the Lord.

"I'm so sorry," she whispered as the shameful truth washed over her. It wasn't about her and Joe after all. It was about Joe and his relationship with the Lord.

Even if he never came back to her, his heart and soul were right back where they belonged.

The revelation filled her with a sense of peace so strong, tears of joy sprang to her eyes.

Are You here, Lord? Is that You I feel beside me?

Until the other night, she'd gone so long without truly feeling God's presence. And like the other night, He was here. He'd never left her. She just needed to clear her head of the selfish thoughts and focus on someone besides herself.

Lisa was amazed at the blessed peace, even stronger than before, as it flowed through her.

For a long time, she sat there and prayed. She prayed prayers of forgiveness, prayers of thanksgiving. But mostly she just rested in Him, knowing He was with her and would see her through every trial she faced. She just needed to keep her eyes firmly fixed on Him.

This was something she had to share with Joe. She rose and turned toward the cabin. Before she could take a step, Joe stepped onto the deck.

The sight of him took her breath away. The easy gentle smile, the hope that lit his eyes. These were all things she never thought she'd see again.

"Joe, I need to apologize to you." Lisa swallowed hard.

"Apologize?"

She nodded. *Please, Lord, give me the right words.*

"I've been thinking only of myself, of getting you to come home. I wasn't considering you at all."

"Of course you were."

"No." She shook her head. "I knew you were hurting over Cody, of course. And I prayed God would ease your pain as well as mine. And I knew you needed to find peace, just like I did. All this was about more than you coming home to me. It was about your returning home to the Lord."

"My relationship with the Lord is getting better."

"No thanks to me. Somewhere along the way, I forgot that's what was important. And I forgot about my *own* relationship with Him. I spouted it, of course, but I didn't feel it. I've been thinking about how wrong I was. How I hurt you rather than helped you."

"You didn't hurt me, Lisa."

"Yes, I did. I'm so sorry. When I accused you of taking your eyes off God, I was really the one who had. I became so focused on getting you to come home to me that I took my eyes off Him and forgot about something I knew in those awful days after Cody first died. You needed to find your way back to God. That's the only way your life will ever be right again. My eyes are back where they belong. They're firmly on the Lord, just like yours are. I can see it. And if you don't come home, at least—"

"Before I do, there's something you should know."

She stared at him for a full minute before she comprehended his words.

"Before you do what?"

"Come home."

"Joe?" *Dare she hope?*

"I never wanted a divorce. I only thought it would be best for you if I was out of your life. I e-mailed Mike the morning we went to Juneau, and told him I'd changed my mind."

"You did?" She stared at him, unsure what to say.

He nodded. "The message you opened from Mike was an old one, replying to one from the *old* me. You probably didn't notice the dates. I really don't like stacked e-mail. It can be so confusing. But if you looked in the *sent* folder, you would have seen the one I sent asking Mike to stop the proceedings."

The hope rising in Lisa's heart terrified her. She couldn't take another letdown where Joe was concerned. Still, she whispered, "What changed your mind?"

"Praying. The more time I spent with Him, the more I changed. But it all started with you. That day you yelled at me...I thought about the things you said to me about taking my eyes off God. About finding the joy in the sorrows. They're all hard things to do. You were doing it alone. I was doing it alone. No wonder we took our eyes off of Him. We were so caught up in blaming ourselves, and we forgot to praise Him for being there to carry us through."

Lisa's heart hurt as she recognized the truth in Joe's words. "That's when we lost our focus. At least, I know I did."

"Me, too," Joe admitted.

"You said you had something to tell me. What is it?"

"I quit my job."

Lisa blinked, not sure she heard him right. "You what?"

"Quit my job."

"Why?"

"I'm a burned-out lawyer who never did enjoy handling divorce cases. I don't really think that's God's plan for me. What more can I say?"

Before Lisa could react, Joe was on one knee with one of her hands tucked between both of his. "How would you like to be a farmer's wife?"

"A farmer's wife? What are you talking about?"

"Jessica's tulip farm. I told her I'd come stay at the farm; take care of it for her while she travels. I said I'd learn the business and then if I like it, I would buy it from her. But I also said I wouldn't do it unless the conditions were right."

"What conditions are those?"

"That you go with me."

"You want me to move? Away from the home we had with our son?" Panic filled her in a sudden grab.

"He's not there, Lisa. He's in heaven with God. He's in our hearts and memories where he'll be forever. But if it makes you feel better, we can try to find a way to keep the house."

Lisa swallowed hard and tried to blink back tears. Unsuccessful, they spilled down her cheeks in a hot trail. She slapped at them, angry with herself for crying in front of Joe. "Sorry," she whispered.

"Ah, Lisa, don't be. Your tears were my problem, never yours. They reminded me of the guilt I felt. Of all the ways I let you and Cody down."

"You didn't. He thought you were the best dad in the world."

"He did?"

Lisa nodded. "That day, on the way to the game, he told me not to be mad at you. He said you had to work hard so you could pay for the trip to Alaska to see the orcas. He said you were the best dad in the world."

Joe swiped at his eyes.

"Thank you. Thank you for telling me that."

She smiled, glad she could give Joe some modicum of peace where their son was concerned.

"You don't have to make a decision about moving

today. Take some time and think about it. But I'd really like you to come with me. Just think about what it will be like in the spring."

They'd been to Skagit Valley when the tulips were in full bloom. It was like nothing she'd ever seen. Fields and fields of color, everywhere she looked. If she closed her eyes, she could picture her and Joe standing in one of those fields with their arms around each other. They would be laughing, soaking in the beauty of it all, their love for each other surrounding them.

"I'll go with you to Jessica's tulip farm on one condition."

He merely smiled at her and raised one brow quizzically.

"We learn the tulip business together. And in the evenings, you have to promise to let me help you get all of your children's stories ready to send to a publisher."

Joe answered her with a kiss that buckled her knees.

"Miss Lisa! Miss Lisa!"

Joe groaned as she pulled away. "It's OK, Joe. There's plenty of time for making up." She turned to Brandon, who danced around her and Joe in delight. "What is it, sweetheart?"

"The whales! They're here! Hurry! The captain said the best view is from the bow. He said they'll come really close to us. Come on. Hurry!" Brandon tugged at her hand, and she let him pull her along. But she kept her other hand firmly on Joe's. He had to come, too.

Together they followed Brandon through the cabin where he prepared to climb a small ladder that led out to the bow.

"Don't forget your life-jacket, Brandon," Chad called out to his son.

Without an argument, Brandon stopped and pulled on an orange vest off a rack near the ladder. He waited until Lisa and Joe followed suit, and then tugged them toward the ladder. After they were out on the bow, he pointed at the ship's rail.

"There," he said proudly. "The captain said we could sit right there and watch them. Cuz it's Cody's birthday and we're special."

Joe leaned down and whispered in Lisa's ear. "He told the captain about Cody and the day you missed the whales."

"You were right yesterday when you said he's something else."

"So are you." Joe pressed a kiss on her neck, just below her ear. "I love you, Lisa."

"Come on you guys." Brandon motioned them over to the wooden railing. "Hurry before some other people come here." Jessica and Chad both made their way to either side of Brandon, which was good because Lisa would have worried about him being so close to the edge in spite of wearing a life jacket.

The rush of air from the water below was cold as they stepped closer to the rail, but Lisa didn't care. She was going to see the whales that her son loved so much.

For Cody.

She caught her first eyeful of shiny black smoothness as the orca leapt out of the water then dove back in with only the slightest splash.

When it popped back up, there were two of them. And as they danced across the water it seemed as if they watched the five of them and performed for them alone. Then they leaped in the air and the show began all over again.

Brandon's shouts and giggles faded away into the background as Lisa's breath caught and her eyes filled with tears of joy. Each time the whales leaped into the air or dove into the water, her heart danced and dove with them. Beside her, Joe grabbed her hand and squeezed tight.

"He's here with us, Lisa. Our little boy is here." He smiled through his tears, and Lisa's heart soared to impossible new heights.

"I know." Her own tears flowed and her throat tightened as she whispered, "Happy Birthday, Cody."

"Happy Birthday, son," Joe echoed. "God is with us, too," he said after a moment.

"I know. I can feel them both right here with us."

"I love you, Lisa."

"I love you, too, Joe." She stood on her tiptoes, leaned over and pressed her lips against his. The boat dipped at that moment and she stumbled. But her mouth never left his.

"Welcome home, Joe" she whispered against his lips as he pulled his arms tightly around her. "Welcome home."

Thank you for purchasing this Harbourlight title. For other inspirational stories, please visit our on-line bookstore at www.pelicanbookgroup.com.

For questions or more information, contact us at customer@pelicanbookgroup.com.

Harbourlight Books
The Beacon in Christian Fiction™
an imprint of Pelican Ventures Book Group
www.pelicanbookgroup.com

May God's glory shine through
this inspirational work of fiction.

AMDG